Northwest Vista College
Learning Resource Center
3535 North Ellison Drive
San Antonio, Texas 78251

D1564454

A Jade in Aries

A Jade in Aries

Donald E. Westlake
writing as Tucker Coe

Five Star
Unity, Maine

Five Star Mystery Series.
Published in 2001 in conjunction with Tekno Books &
Ed Gorman.

The text of this edition is unabridged.

Set in 11 pt. Plantin.

Printed in the United States on permanent paper.

Library of Congress Cataloging-in-Publication Data

Coe, Tucker.
    A jade in Aries / by Donald E. Westlake writing as Tucker
Coe.
      p. cm.
    "A Mitchel Tobin mystery" — Cover.
    ISBN 0-7862-3015-0 (hc : alk. paper)
    1. Tobin, Mitch (Fictitious character) — Fiction.
    2. Private investigators — New York (State) — New York —
Fiction. 3. New York (N.Y.) — Fiction. I. Title.
PS3573.E9 J34 2001
813'.54—dc21   2001018151

For the Hand
of the
Four-in-Hand

Introducing Tucker Coe
by Donald E. Westlake

The first few years I was writing, I produced far too much. If I'd been a little older I might have burned out, but as it was, I just kept finding new areas to explore, new ways to write, new subjects, new formats. I was like a kid who's just moved into a new neighborhood and won't be content until he's run through every new alley, climbed over every new fence, surveyed every inch of this new world.

All of that exuberance peaked in 1965, when I published twelve short stories, in magazines from *Playboy* to *Ellery Queen's Mystery Magazine*. The stories were all over the lot: mystery, science fiction, comedy, slices of life. In addition, Westlake wrote a novel, *The Spy in the Ointment* (I've always hated that title), and so did Richard Stark. But Stark, after eight novels about his character Parker, wrote *The Damsel*, his first novel without Parker, featuring Parker's associate Alan Grofield. And a new fellow, more short-lived, weighed in, one Curt Clark, with a science fiction novel, *Anarchaos*.

In addition to all that published work, I also scampered down some blind alleys, putting together two anthology ideas that nobody wanted, plus three movie treatments that nobody wanted (at that time, I still thought the word for those things was "outline") and two television series treatments that nobody wanted, one of which later became trans-mogrified into a novel of mine called *Help I'm Being Held Prisoner*.

The following year, 1966, at last I began to slow down, but at the same time I continued to expand. I wrote no short stories that year, no unwanted treatments, no unassembled anthologies (but one published anthology, my only, *Once Against the Law*, done with William Tenn). All I did that year was three novels, a Westlake (*God Save the Mark*), a Stark about Parker (*The Rare Coin Score*) and another brand-new guy, Tucker Coe.

In a way, Tucker Coe came out of my desire to unlearn something I'd perhaps learned a bit too well. When I was 14 or 15, I'd read *The Thin Man* (my first Hammett), and it was an astonishing read, I believe the single most important learning experience of my career. It was a sad, lonely, lost book, but it pretended to be cheerful and aware and full of good fellowship.

I hadn't known it was possible to do that, to seem to be saying one thing while you really said a different thing or even the opposite. It was three-dimensional writing, like three-dimensional chess, a writing style you could look through like water and glimpse the fish swimming by underneath. Nabokov was the other master of that, but Hammett I read first.

Much of the technique involved suffusing the story with emotions without mentioning the emotions. (Peter Rabe had that strength, too.) One way and another, I'd been trying to do something similar in my own early books and stories. Then, when comedy came in, that altered the situation, because comedy blankets emotion like radio interference. And Stark, of course, was poker-faced by definition. But wasn't it sometimes a good idea *not* to cloak the emotions?

8

Was I letting one approach to story and character muffle me?

Tucker Coe came out of that. Mitch Tobin is a guy who's hurting so much, and so freshly, that he can't hide his emotions even though he desperately wants to. That was an interesting thing to try to do, write in such a way that the fish would break the surface sometimes.

Now, thirty-five years later, I can't remember how I came up with this particular character with this particular problem, but I do know I started out wanting to write a *mystery*, a story in which the hero solves a murder, or series of murders. Since I was never content to just ride the road already traveled, but always wanted to twist the concept or embellish it or alter it somehow, this time the idea was that the detective was reluctant to *be* a detective, because he had serious problems of his own that consumed all his attention. (I realize now, somewhat after the fact, that even in this I was echoing *The Thin Man*, in which Nick Charles is extremely reluctant to think about the disappearance of Clyde Wynant, having to be repeatedly prodded and nagged by Nora to get on with it.)

I liked Mitch Tobin, and I learned from him, but I'm afraid his end was in his beginning. The whole point with him was that the hurt was fresh. Over the next six years, I wrote a total of five novels about Mitch Tobin, but partway through the last of them, *Don't Lie to Me*, I realized I wouldn't be able to write about him any more, not after that book. Emotional wounds heal, or they fester and turn rank. Mitch had to get over his trauma one way or another. If he finally accepted himself so he could move on with his life, he'd be just another private eye, and no longer of interest to me. If on the other hand he became neurotic, stuck in the past, he might be interesting to psychiatrists, but not to me. I didn't kill him off, I didn't see any need to go that far, but at the end of that final book I let him sleep.

One last note, about the pen name. My first editor at Random House, through the sixties, was Lee Wright, known as the Queen of the mystery. A wonderful person and a fantastic editor, I learned a lot from her. She had little professional crotchets, however, such as refusing to let anybody use the word "dead" in a title (her only taboo word), so that the book I wanted to call *The Dead Nephew*, for instance, because I think the word "nephew" is comic, became called *The Fugitive Pigeon* instead, which is another title I've always hated. And never understood.

But that's a digression. Lee Wright's attitude toward pseudonyms was that the most memorable kind of moniker was a perfectly ordinary last name coupled with an unusual first name (Carter Brown, Cordwainer Smith, Marco Page). In the mid-sixties, I was a New York Giants football fan, and their running backs in those years were a couple guys named Ernie Koy and Tucker Fredericksen, so I said, "How about Tucker Koy?" Lee said, "I'm not sure why, but Tucker Koy sounds obscene." So he became Tucker Coe.

If it is possible to be neutral about a subject such as astrology, I am neutral. None of the characters in this book expresses my opinion on the subject, primarily because I have no opinion. In my personal head, astrology is filed—along with the Tarot deck, the I Ching and a dozen other pre-scientific disciplines—in the drawer labeled MAYBE. For those interested in the subject, the natal horoscopes in this book are legitimate, drawn up for dates and places of birth chosen at random. The progressed readings were chosen for their applicability to the plot, but all are possible for those natal horoscopes at one time or another.

The birth information on the principal characters in this book:

Ronald Cornell	Atlanta, Georgia	August 25, 1939	7:20 P.M.
Jamie Dearborn	Omaha, Nebraska	April 11, 1942	6:10 A.M.
Henry Koberberg	New York, N.Y.	July 12, 1933	9:15 A.M.
Cary Lane	Los Angeles, Calif.	February 3, 1941	10:00 P.M.
Bruce Maundy	New York, N.Y.	March 28, 1943	11:25 P.M.
David Poumon	Toronto, Ont., Can.	June 5, 1945	10:35 A.M.
Stewart Remington	New York, N.Y.	April 22, 1929	3:15 A.M.
Leo Ross	Long Island, N.Y.	February 27, 1937	11:55 A.M.
Jerry Weissman	Frankfurt, Germany	Nov. 26, 1950	2:20 P.M.

Again, this book is meant neither as an attack upon astrology nor as a defense of astrology, but only as a fiction to be—I hope—enjoyed.

Tucker Coe
February, 1970

11

1

I was in the basement, digging, when Ronald Cornell first appeared. I was alone in the house—Bill was at school and Kate was off to her part-time job in the department store—and the first I knew he was there was when a soft male voice called down the cellar stairs, "Hello? Is anyone home?"

For just a second I felt a chill up my back that had more to do with the irrational fears of childhood than anything else. I was standing knee-deep in a freshly dug hole, my surroundings as poorly lit by bare bulbs as most basements, and a stranger had suddenly appeared at the head of the stairs—the only exit.

From where I was, I couldn't see him. I automatically took a tighter grip on the shovel as I called, "What is it?"

"Mr. Tobin? Mr. Mitchell Tobin?"

Wasn't this the way people used to be called to Heaven—or to Hell—in those horror movies I used to see on Saturday afternoons as a boy? Aware of the foolishness of my reaction, but stupidly unable to do anything about it, I shouted, more forcefully than I'd intended, *"What do you want?"*

He started down the stairs. My view was from the far wall across the open stairs, so I could see as much of him as was below the level of the basement ceiling, and what came into sight first were his shoes; they were brown, with brass buckles. Leather and metal both gleamed in the yellow light.

He was saying, in his soft and frail-sounding voice, "I'm sorry to bother you. I rang the bell. The door wasn't locked, so I thought perhaps there was something wrong."

His trousers were plaid, in shades of green and brown. They flared below the knee. It was snowing out—this was January 7th, winter's fist was firmly clenched—but there was no sign of bad weather on his shoes or trousers. Nor on the dark green silk socks that showed between.

I stepped up out of the hole, but kept my grip on the shovel. There was nothing rational in my mind at all, nothing but confusion.

His jacket was tan, a bit darker than the usual color of camel's-hair coats, and seemed to be of some very soft material, like cashmere. It was fitted very tightly at the waist, and flared out below, making him look as though he had large soft hips.

There were simple wooden railings on both sides of the staircase, and now his hand appeared, resting on the rail nearer me. Like everything else about him, the hand was soft-looking, the fingers somewhat thick and blunt. Emerging from the end of his jacket sleeve, over his wrist, was a ruffled white lace shirt cuff.

Only a few seconds had gone by since he'd started down the stairs, and he continued to talk as he came: "I hope you don't mind my barging in like this. I suppose I should have called first, but I was afraid you'd say no, and I really am desperate."

Desperate? He didn't *sound* desperate. Or was I, filled with my own foolish first impressions, simply unable to hear the overtones in his voice?

He wore a fluffy ascot, in shades of rust and green. But now he had descended far enough for me to see his face, and all at once I knew who—or that is to say what—he was. I leaned the shovel against the cement wall, and took a step toward him.

I was never assigned to the Vice Squad, but in the course of my eighteen years as a New York City cop I had inevitably gotten to know quite a bit about the local homosexual community: the more common stereotypes in which they appear, and the kinds of individuals who prey upon them.

My visitor was a type I recognized at once; what I thought of as the Bruised. Slender, weak-looking, with a delicate round head that was balding in a way he surely found embarrassing, he wore the (habitual?) self-deprecating apologetic smile of the person who doesn't expect anyone else to take his pain seriously. This is the kind of queer that is found beaten and robbed in parks, in public restrooms and empty alleys; they seldom want to press charges, even on those rare occasions when their attacker is picked up. Occasionally they are found dead. Something in them, perhaps their very vulnerability, so palpable and total, seems to evoke a wild savagery in their attackers, and the deaths are often terrible.

But the clothing was all wrong for the pattern. This type, the Bruised, is normally employed as a clerk in some large corporation or somewhere in Civil Service, and dresses appropriately in drab conservatism. This one's clothing belonged to a different category entirely; what a friend of mine on the force used to call the Creative Queen. I wasn't sufficiently knowledgeable on the subject to be sure, but from my television talk-show viewing I thought it a safe guess that my visitor's clothing was as current and "in" as it was possible to be.

He was saying, as he reached the bottom of the stairs, "Please forgive me if I seem pushy. I just didn't know where else to turn."

I said, "What did you want?" I was feeling irritable now, partly at having been interrupted in my digging, partly at having so foolishly frightened myself, and I made no attempt

14

to keep my annoyance out of my voice.

He began to blink, very rapidly, and to flutter his hands in front of himself. "I'm sorry," he said. "If I'm interrupting—I'll come back if it would be better—I don't mean to, I know you're busy." And he gestured vaguely at the hole behind me.

I had forgotten how easy it was to panic people like this. Homosexuals of the Bruised type usually are the result of a violently dominating father, and they tend to crumple at any demonstration of harsh authority. I was immediately embarrassed at what I'd done, and tried to make amends. "I'm digging a sub-basement," I said, feeling the need to explain myself. "For storage. There's no rush on it."

"I could come back another time," he said. One buckled shoe was already back up on the lowest step.

"No, you're here now. What's the problem?"

"Thank you." He tried a tentative smile, but kept on blinking. "Uh—Well." The frightened smile flashed on and off again. "Now that I'm here, I don't know where to start."

"With your name," I suggested.

"Oh, I'm terribly sorry! My name's Ronald Cornell. I live on Remsen Street, over in Brooklyn Heights?"

"I know where it is."

"Yes. I have a little shop over there. A male boutique?" He tended, I could see, to make statements as though they were questions. People who live in two worlds—immigrants, homosexuals, some criminal types, some show-business types—often develop that mannerism as a result of talking so often to people outside their own tight sphere.

"A men's clothing store," I said now, to show him I understood what a male boutique was. (I also understood now the contradiction between his face and his clothing.)

"Something like that," he said, and I nodded to indicate I

15

understood that there were undoubtedly crucial differences between a male boutique and a men's clothing store. "My place," he said, "is called Jammer?"

"I'm afraid I don't know it."

"It's just a little neighborhood shop," he said, as though that were the reason.

"You have a problem with the store?" I couldn't understand yet what he was doing here.

"No, it's my—" The blinking started again, more violently than before, and an expression of remembered agony dragged his face into downward arcs. "My partner," he said.

"In the store?"

"Yes. Everywhere."

He hadn't made that one a question, but I nodded anyway. "I understand. What about him? What's his name?"

"Jamie. Jamie Dearbuh—" He shook his head. "I'm sorry, forgive me. His name is Dearborn. Jamie Dearborn." And he looked at me with such desolation that I suddenly realized there had to be death in it somewhere. Nothing else gives human eyes quite that expression of loss.

I said, as gently as I could, "What happened?"

"He said it was the Changeable Sailor. Is that a police term?"

"The Changeable Sailor? I never heard the phrase before."

"I wasn't sure if he'd made it up or not," he said, and gave a quick nervous smile that made no sense.

I said, "Who made it up? Jamie?"

"No, the detective." He shook his head, the nervous smile twitching on and off, and made vague indefinite movements with his hands. "I'm sorry, I know I'm saying this all wrong, you don't have any idea what I'm talking about. It's just that I don't want to say the main thing, you see, that's what it is, about Jamie being, you know, dead." He looked away from me, smiling blindly at the stairs.

I said, "When did this happen?"

"Last weekend. Saturday."

Today was Wednesday; no wonder the wound was still fresh. I said, "The police say a sailor did it?"

"No. Not exactly." His hands folded across his waist, and the fingers of his right hand began to twitch at the lace over his left wrist. Head down, watching his fingers move, he said, "I wish he could explain it to you himself. Manzoni. Detective Manzoni." He looked quickly at me. "Do you know him?"

"No, I don't. What was it he said about the sailor?"

"He said—" Cornell looked down at his twitching fingers again, and talked to them. "He said it happens all the time. He said a sailor gets off a ship in New York, he's been weeks or months at sea, he's only got one night on shore, and he wants a woman. So he goes to bars, and he drinks, and he doesn't find a woman, and finally a—someone tries to pick him up. Some boy." A quick look at me, and away. "Some homosexual, you see."

"Yes," I said. I knew where the story was going.

"And the sailor," he went on, "decides to go with the boy. Because he can't find a woman, and he doesn't want his time on shore to be a complete waste, and something is better than nothing. And they go to the boy's place, or somewhere else, somewhere private, and then the sailor changes his mind and gets mad because things didn't work out the way he wanted, and he takes it out on the boy. He beats up the boy. And sometimes he kills him."

"Yes," I said.

"That's what he called the Changeable Sailor," Cornell said. "Manzoni did."

"A good enough name for him," I said. "That kind of thing does happen."

"But not to Jamie!" Cornell cried, and was suddenly staring directly at me, all his pain on the surface. "To *me*, that could happen to *me* if I didn't have—if Jamie hadn't come into—But not to *him*." He scrabbled into his inside jacket pocket, saying, "Here, look at this. You'll see. It isn't possible, it just isn't possible."

He came out at last with a page torn from some glossy magazine, folded over twice. Hurriedly, but almost reverently, he unfolded it and handed it over. His eyes were shining.

I took the page and looked at it. It was a full-page ad from a clothing manufacturer, for the same style of apparel as that being worn by Cornell. The bottom quarter of the ad had copy, black lettering on white, but the top three quarters was a full-color photograph of a young man standing in a dramatic pose on a huge boulder in a field. In the background, a herd of horses was running pell-mell from right to left.

The young man was a Negro, with very light skin: milk-chocolate. He was lean and graceful, with the body and stance of a dancer. His face was handsome, firm-jawed, strong looking, and at the same time quite obviously homosexual. His hair was worn in the natural style lately popular, but not to any wild excess.

This was the Creative Queen, this was the one for whom this clothing was made. The difference between Ronald Cornell, fidgeting awkwardly and looking both forlorn and ridiculous in his finery, and the young man in this photograph, who wore the equivalent finery as naturally and appropriately as any cavalier, was cruel and complete.

I looked up from the picture to see Cornell gazing hopefully at me, his expression for some reason expectant. Then I understood; the lover awaiting admiration for his beloved.

I said, "This is Jamie?"

"You see it's not possible," he said. "You see he wouldn't pick up a *sailor*."

"Or anyone else? Did he never do anything like that?"

"Jamie?" I handed him back the picture; he turned it so he could look at it, and said, "Jamie could have anybody he wanted. He didn't have to go after strangers, they all wanted Jamie." He looked at me again and shook his head. "Jamie never cruised," he said. "He never did."

"All right." I thought I knew now what it was all about, and I said, "But I suppose this Detective . . ."

"Manzoni."

"Yes. I suppose he's satisfied with his sailor theory, and isn't looking around for anybody else."

"He isn't doing *anything*. He says it's hopeless, and he isn't even *trying*."

I took a deep breath, and said, "Before you go any further, let me explain a couple of things to you. I used to be on the police force, I'm not any more."

"I know that."

"I don't have a license to practice as a private detective," I said. "If I were to try to do Manzoni's job, I could get into very serious trouble."

"Oh, no," he said. "That isn't what I want. No, that's up to me. I wouldn't expect anyone else to do it. I have to find Jamie's murderer myself."

I frowned at him. "Then what do you want from me?"

He got fidgety again, but this time it seemed to be more embarrassment than emotion. He said, "I don't know if you put much credence in astrology."

"Astrology?" Now what?

19

Donald E. Westlake

"Well, it doesn't matter," he said. "I wouldn't try to convert anybody. The point is, what I need to know is people's birthdays. And not just the date, but the exact *time* of their birth. It's on everybody's birth certificate, what time you were born."

"I'm not following you," I said. "What do you need this information for?"

"Well, if you don't believe in astrology you'll probably think I'm foolish."

"I won't think anything," I said. "I just want to understand what you have in mind."

"Well," he said, "it will be in the stars, won't it? I mean, if all the important things in our lives are in the stars, recorded in the stars, then the murder will be there too, won't it?"

"You're going to find the murderer through astrology?"

"I have to try," he said. "What else can I do?"

I shook my head. What he was saying was nonsense, of course, but what else *could* he do? The New York City Police Department, like every other facet of municipal government, is understaffed and overworked. Detective Manzoni was merely following the line of least resistance in assuming that a normal pattern of violence held true in this case. If what Manzoni called the Changeable Sailor really was the murderer—as in most cases like this he in fact was—then there was nothing Manzoni could do, and he would be justified in filing the case in the Open file and forgetting it. I would be tempted to do the same thing myself, were I still on the force.

So what were the choices open to Ronald Cornell? There'd be no point in his trying to get any more action out of the police by going over Manzoni's head; the detective on the case wasn't likely to be reversed by his superiors without a great deal of solid evidence against him, and particularly not

20

when the complainant was an obvious homosexual, against whom official bias would be subtle, unacknowledged and inevitable.

Jamie Dearborn had obviously been vitally important in Cornell's life; no doubt Cornell had never expected to land so enviable a "partner," and knew it would never happen to him again. There would be no more Jamies in Cornell's life. So how could he do nothing about the loss of Jamie? And where there was nothing rational to be done, that left only the irrational. He would find Jamie's murderer through astrology; the name would be found written among the stars.

It wouldn't be, of course, and eventually Cornell would have to give up the idea. In the meantime, though, it seemed harmless. It would give him something to do while learning to forget, and it would keep him from a futile assault against City Hall.

So I didn't argue with him about his plan. Let him occupy himself in busywork; wasn't my own life built on the same irrational soil? Wasn't I digging this sub-cellar? Wasn't I, when the weather was better, working on my wall?

I said, "I still don't see what you want me to do."

"I asked around," he said. "I was told about you, that you used to be on the police force. I thought you would know how I could find out the birthdays. I don't know how to go about it."

"You need date and time of birth?"

"Yes. It's always on the birth certificate."

"I know that. How many people?"

"Six."

I looked at him in astonishment. "You have it narrowed to six?"

"Yes. I made a list of the suspects, and found out who had alibis, and these six are left."

"How did you make a list of suspects?"

"Well, it had to be somebody that Jamie knew. He was very careful about letting people into the apartment, he would never have let a stranger in. Not even the grocery boy, he'd make him leave the package in the foyer. He'd put the chain on the door, and open it just enough to give him the tip."

"So you made a list of people Jamie would have let in."

"Yes."

"How many?"

"Fourteen."

"And eight of them had alibis."

"Yes."

"You've done all this in four days?"

"Two days, actually," he said. "I didn't start until Monday, when I finally saw that Detective Manzoni wasn't going to do anything."

I was taken aback. Cornell had gone about his investigation in the most professional way possible; listing the potential suspects on the basis of the habits of the victim, eliminating from the list on the basis of alibi. And now he was going to make a direct about-face into the irrational.

I felt the terrible temptation to become involved. But I wasn't going to, I was going to stay completely out of it. Not only because of the problem of a private detective's license, but also because I had enough pain of my own, I didn't need to envelop myself in someone else's agony.

What Cornell hadn't realized yet was this: Even if he did find Jamie Dearborn's murderer, even if he managed to obtain convictable evidence (as astrological charts, of course, would not be), even if he somehow got the murderer arrested and convicted and jailed, even then Jamie Dearborn would go on being dead. Cornell didn't really want vengeance, I could see that in his eyes. What he wanted was his partner back, alive and well. But that was the one thing he was not going to get, no matter what he did, and when all the activity was done, he was going to have to face it. That moment would be terrible, and I had no desire to be present.

So I made no suggestions, I made no offers. I simply said, "All right, you have six suspects. Were they all born in New York?"

He looked surprised. "I really don't know. Of course, I'll have to know that too, won't I?"

"Naturally."

"Yes, I should have thought of that. Location on the planet is just as important as time, astrologically."

"That isn't what I meant," I said. "Birth certificates are maintained in the county where you were born, so we'll have to know the counties before we can get the certificates."

"Oh, of course." He frowned, and said thoughtfully, "I know some of them. I suppose I might be able to find out the others. Would it be imposing too much to use your phone?"

"Not at all," I said. "Let's go upstairs."

"Thank you." He stepped back to let me go first up the stairs.

I was still wearing my work gloves, which I now stripped off and dropped on the floor before going up. We went silently up to the kitchen, where I said, "I'll wash up out here. The phone's in the living room."

"Thank you very much." He paused, looking awkward, and said, "I really appreciate this."

"I haven't done anything yet," I said.

"You didn't dismiss me out of hand," he said, and flashed his embarrassed smile, and went on into the living room.

I washed at the kitchen sink, fully realizing now what a study in contrasts we must have been down in the basement, he so neat and so elegantly turned out, me in ripped old sneakers, paint-stained trousers, frayed flannel shirt and work gloves, my face and forearms smeared with dirt and perspiration. I felt an urge to go upstairs and change into cleaner clothes, but of course as soon as Cornell left I would go back to my digging.

Above the kitchen sink was a window facing the back yard. Out there it was still grim, snowflakes endlessly dropping like miniature parachutists down through the windless air, making anonymous mounds of my wall and the canvas-covered stacks of matériel waiting for spring.

I have been working on my wall now for close to two years. The work is its own purpose, so I have seen to it that the job goes very slowly. When completed, the wall will be ten feet high and two feet thick, composed of brick and concrete block, built on a solid concrete-block footing that extends into the earth below the frost line. There will be no windows or doors or other openings in the wall, which will completely enclose the yard on three sides. The house itself will form the fourth wall, so that when I am finished the only entrance to the yard will be through the house.

The wall is now about four feet high all the way around. I am progressing slowly, but no matter how slowly I move, the wall continues toward completion. Some day it will be finished, which I don't like to think about.

Last winter, the second winter since I was thrown off the force and the first winter since I started the wall, was a very difficult time. I couldn't work on my wall during January and February, and I had nothing else to do but sit in front of the television set all day, hoping the movements on the screen would distract me from thoughts of where I was and how I had put myself here. This winter the idea came to me to give myself a second project, indoors, to carry me through the time of worst weather. So I am digging a sub-basement. Beginning at the rear wall of the house, I intend to first dig a flight of steps down to a depth of eight feet. Then I will dig a room out of the earth under the concrete floor of the basement. I will be careful not to dig under any of the structural supports of the house, and I will erect firm supports for the basement floor as I dig. This project may last much longer than the wall, and give me a much longer respite from myself.

Once, in the first year after I was thrown off the force, I dreamed that Jock called me on the phone. Though he spoke to me at length, I couldn't seem to make out any of the words. But the astonishing thing was that he didn't sound angry, and when I awoke in the morning I felt both pleasure and amazement at the memory. I almost said to Kate, "Jock isn't mad at me, isn't that incredible?" But I realized in time that it was only a dream.

I find it difficult to describe what I did, to put it in words; I tend to talk in circles around it. How fast can I say it, in how few words? My partner, Detective Jock Sheehan, was shot to death because, instead of being at his side, I was in bed with a woman other than my wife. Oh, but there's even more to it than that. Jock knew where I was, the affair had been going on for four years and he had helped me keep it going and keep it quiet. And the woman, Linda Campbell, was the wife of a jailed burglar I had arrested. How do I betray thee, self? Let me count the ways.

It is to keep myself from counting the ways that I work on my wall, and that now, in the dead of winter, I dig a hole beneath my basement.

The water was running in the sink. I had been staring out the window at the gray air, the white snow, how long? Sometimes I think I will stop like that once and never start again;

and in many ways, that would be best.

I shook my head, and turned off the water, and dried my arms and hands and face on a towel. Over by the cellar door were my slippers. I went over there, kicked off the muddy sneakers, and put the slippers on. Not to track dirt on Kate's carpets.

I heard Cornell talking in the living room as I came down the hall. He was sitting perched on the edge of the sofa, talking into the phone. He had a silver pen in his hand and a notebook open on the end table. He was saying, "Yes, well, one has to go on, doesn't one?" And then a pause, and, "Oh, not till next week. The thought of the shop without Jamie, not yet. I'll open next Monday." Another pause, and, "You are sweet. Everyone's been so kind. I'll see you Friday, then. Yes. *Ciao.*"

He hung up and turned to me. His movements seemed more effeminate when he was sitting down. He said, happily, "I got them. I knew some, and I got the others."

"Fine."

"Here's the list."

I took the notebook from him and looked at the names and locations. "This one in Toronto might take a little longer, I'm not sure."

"Oh, God, I've got time. That's all I have."

"Three of them are New York."

"That's right."

"Which borough?"

"Oh, dear." He stood up beside me to look at the names. "Stew I'm not sure about," he said. "Is it important?"

"It would be easier, but it isn't vital."

"It just might be a little tricksy to ask. Now, Bruce was born in Queens, I know that for a fact. Here, you want the pen?"

"Thank you." I wrote "Queens County" after the name Bruce Maundy.

"And Henry," he said, "I'm not sure about either. I *think* he was born in Manhattan, you know, Lower East Side, but I wouldn't swear to it."

I nodded, and wrote "Manhattan?" after the name Henry Koberberg. "I'll see what I can do," I said, and sat down where Cornell had been sitting.

As I reached for the phone, he said, "We haven't talked about money yet."

"Money?" I looked up at him, not understanding.

"I understood that you sometimes do police-type things," he said, "but of course you have to be paid."

"This isn't anything to be paid for," I said. "I'll make one phone call, that's all."

"Oh, but that isn't right. I came here a perfect stranger, you can't do it for nothing."

I didn't want pay. It is true that from time to time in the last few years I've taken on jobs that had some connection with my police training and abilities, but I've done the work reluctantly, finding the contact with other people painful. But I've had no other way to make a living; how could I expose myself by filling out a normal employer's application form? And how can I allow Kate to support me forever?

But those jobs were difficult, and took considerable time, and I received fairly high sums of money. Even if I wanted to charge for making one phone call to an old friend, how much would be a proper price? Ten cents?

So I said, "I'm not doing enough to charge you. If you want, I'll stop in the store sometime and you can give me a tie or something."

He looked doubtful, knowing I didn't intend ever to come to him for a tie, and said, "I just don't feel right about it."

"Let me make the phone call," I said, "and then we'll talk."

"All right," he said, reluctantly, and stood frowning at me as I called the Missing Persons Bureau.

Eddie Schultz didn't answer, but he was on duty now and they switched the call to his desk. "Mitch Tobin here," I said, and he said, "Hey, Mitch, how you doing?"

"Fine," I said. I haven't seen Eddie for nearly three years, but we'd been friends for fifteen years or so before that, and he was one of the ones who didn't turn against me after Jock was killed.

Now he said, "What can I do for you, Mitch?"

I said, "I have six names, and places of birth. What I want is date and time of birth on each of them. Could you do it for me?"

"Date and *time?*"

"Yes."

"Local?"

"Four local, one Los Angeles, one Canada."

"So you want birth certificates."

"I don't need the actual certificates, just the information."

"Mitch, are you working again?" Once before I'd called him, in connection with one of the jobs I'd taken.

"Not really," I said.

"You don't want to get yourself in trouble."

"I'm careful," I said. "And this is just to be passed on to a friend."

"Okay. Give me the stuff."

I read him the six names and the six places. When I was done, he said, "Some of these I could have tomorrow. The LA and Toronto will take a little longer. You want them all together?"

"Yes."

"Give me a call Monday."

"Is it okay if my friend calls you direct? Cut out the middleman."

"Sure," he said.

"Thanks, Eddie. His name is Ronald Cornell."

He repeated the name, and said, "Tell him to call before eleven. In the morning."

"I will. Thanks a lot, Eddie."

"Any time. Mitch?"

"Yes?"

"Otherwise, how are you?"

"Pretty good," I said.

"You come out of the house at all?"

"Not very much."

"Give me a social call sometime, will you?"

"I will," I promised. "Thanks again."

"Sure thing, Mitch."

We hung up, and I wrote Eddie's name and phone number in Cornell's notebook. Giving it to him, I said, "Call him Monday, before eleven in the morning. He's expecting you."

"Thank you," he said. "I appreciate this, I really do."

I got to my feet. "But you saw how easy it was. I'd be embarrassed to take money for it."

"You must come to the shop," he said. "I insist on that."

"I will," I said.

He thanked me some more, and then he got ready to leave. And now I saw why he'd arrived with no sign of snowstorm on him; he'd removed his outerwear just inside the front door, before finding me in the basement. If the house had been empty, obviously, he'd intended to wait.

The buckled shoes disappeared first, inside knee-high brown leather boots that zipped up the side, enclosing both the shoes and the flared bottoms of his trousers. He then put on an ankle-length dark brown coat in a trench-coat style, but with a fur collar and brass buttons, and topped it all with a hat that looked like an outsized baseball cap, brim and all, made entirely of dark brown fur. After all that, the gloves he took from his coat pocket and pulled on were almost disappointing in their ordinariness.

"Well," he said, "ready to brave the elements. Thank you again, Mr. Tobin, you were really very kind."

"I did nothing at all," I said. I reached for the doorknob to let him out, but then stopped and said, "I wonder if you've thought about what you'll do afterwards."

He frowned at me. "I'm not sure I understand."

"Let's say you find him," I said. "Let's say you narrow it down to one person, astrologically. You can't take astrological charts to court, or to a police station. What if you become convinced it was one particular person, but you don't have any proof to back up the stars?"

"Then I'll have to look for proof," he said, as though it were as simple as that.

I said, "The reason I'm asking, I wouldn't want to have helped you if you were planning to take the law into your own hands."

"Revenge?" His smile was both astonished and bitter. "Me? Go out and beat somebody up, *kill* somebody? Oh, Mr. Tobin, you don't have to worry about *me*, I won't do anything *effective* at all."

That self-hatred of his could turn violent; I considered telling him so, warning him to be on guard before he *did* do something "effective," but I knew he would neither understand nor believe me, so I said nothing about it, only, "In that case, I wish you luck."

"Thank you again," he said, and I opened the door, and he left.

The front door has a window in it. Looking through it, I watched Cornell go cautiously down the snowy stoop and out through the deep snow toward his car, a blue Corvette. His car, or Jamie Dearborn's?

He reminded me of somebody, going away through the snow, stepping high and cautious, wearing his boots and his long coat and his fur collar and that fur hat, a long slender dark figure surrounded by snow.

And then I realized who it was: Greta Garbo, in *Anna Karenina*. I smiled to myself, wondering if Cornell would be pleased at the image. I thought he probably would.

He got into the car, and a moment later it drove slowly away. I turned from the door and went back to the kitchen, where I changed again to the muddy sneakers and went back downstairs to the basement.

Two days later, Friday, a package came for me in the mail. Kate was home, then, and watched me curiously as I opened it and took out a tan cashmere scarf. "That's beautiful," she said, and reached out to touch it.

It was beautiful; soft, delicate, clearly expensive.

She said, "Who is it from?"

There was a small note: "Thank you. Ronald Cornell."

I hadn't told Kate about Cornell, but now we sat together at the kitchen table and I described Wednesday's meeting to her. When I finished, she said, "He didn't want you to do anything else? Help him find the murderer?"

"No," I said. "He didn't ask."

Kate has been strongly in favor of those few jobs I've done the last couple of years, not because they've eased our financial problems but because she believes that if I only remain active in the world I will sooner or later become my old self again. I won't, that old self was buried with Jock, but nothing will destroy her hope.

Now she said, "Maybe he'll come back if the astrology doesn't help."

"I doubt it," I said. "I think I've heard the last of Ronald Cornell."

She reached out to touch the scarf again. "That was really very nice of him," she said.

"Yes, it was," I said.

2

We were eating breakfast together, when Kate said, "Wasn't his name Cornell?" She was reading the *Daily News* at the time.

This was Tuesday, six days after my only meeting with Ronald Cornell. I said, "Yes. Ronald Cornell. He's in the paper?"

"He tried to kill himself."

I frowned. "Let me see."

Kate handed the paper over to me, and I looked at the item. It was back with the A&S ads, under the headline

B'KLYN HEIGHTS STORE
OWNER SUICIDE TRY:

In critical condition at Flatbush Crown Hospital is Ronald Cornell, 185 Remsen Street, Brooklyn, following a fall from a building roof termed by police "an obvious suicide attempt."

Cornell, part owner of Jammer, popular male boutique in the Brooklyn Heights area, made his leap from the roof of 1212 Hicks Streets, where the store is located. Friends say Cornell has been despondent since the unsolved slaying recently of his partner in the boutique enterprise, James Dearborn, with whom Cornell also shared his apartment.

Police say the leap from the roof of the four-story

building occurred at approximately nine P.M. Monday. Clotheslines, the wooden roof of a storage shed, and the bolts of cloth maintained within the shed all helped to cushion Cornell's fall, according to police, who say that the promptness of a neighbor in phoning for assistance also contributed to saving Cornell's life.

No charges have as yet been preferred against Cornell, who remains in a coma and under guard at the hospital, where prognosis by doctors is fair.

Yesterday evening. Yesterday morning he was to have called Eddie Schultz; I wondered if he had.

Kate, seeing that I was done reading, said, "Isn't that terrible?"

"Yes, it is," I said, and handed the paper back to her.

She looked at it again, and shook her head. "Why would anybody do a thing like that?"

I knew why it might be done, might be thought of, but I said nothing.

Kate looked at me. "He didn't act suicidal when you saw him last week?"

"That wasn't suicide," I said. "Somebody tried to kill him."

Startled, she glanced down again at the newspaper, and then back up at me. "Kill? Do you really think so?"

"I'm sure of it," I said.

"Because his partner was killed? But he *was* despondent over that, wasn't he?"

"Yes, he was. But if he was going to kill himself, he wouldn't do it that way."

She frowned. "Why not?"

"Two reasons. One psychological, one physical. Psychologically, Ronald Cornell would never kill himself in a way that would cause him pain or leave him ugly. He might take

34

poison, he'd be more likely to turn on the gas. But he wouldn't jump off a roof."

"You can't say that, though. Under emotional stress people always act differently."

"With more intensity," I said, "but not out of character."

She looked dubious. "What's the other reason?"

"The physical details are wrong," I said. "Read that news item again. He landed on a wooden shed full of bolts of cloth. It doesn't say whether he jumped off the front of the building or the back, but a storage shed wouldn't be in front, so it had to be the back."

"I assumed it was, yes." She looked from the paper to me again.

"I know that part of Brooklyn Heights," I said. "There aren't any front lawns there. There's the street, the sidewalk and the building front. If he'd gone off the front, there would have been nothing to break his fall but the sidewalk."

"That could be just accident," she said. "He went up on the roof, and he was distressed, and he just turned the nearest way."

"Except that his store's in that building. That storage shed and those bolts of cloth have to have something to do with the store. It has to be *his* cloth."

Now her frown changed, and she said, "Oh, I see."

"A man wanting to kill himself," I said, "doesn't jump onto bolts of cloth. Not when there's sidewalk on the other side of the building. And no matter how distressed he was, if he'd gone up on that roof planning to kill himself—and I still say he wouldn't have done it that way—he would have remembered that in *this* direction is certain death on the side-walk, but in *that* direction is only possible death because of his own storage shed full of his own stock of cloth."

She said, "Then what do you think happened?"

"I think he was hit on the head," I said. "While he was in

35

the store, probably. Then he was carried up to the roof. The murderer didn't take him to the front because he was afraid somebody in the street below might see him. That's the only explanation for Cornell's body going off the back."

She said, "But couldn't it be one of those cases where somebody tries to kill himself but doesn't really want to? Doesn't that happen?"

"It happens more often than real suicide," I said. "It's a way of getting the world to pay attention to your problems. But that false-start kind of thing is done under completely different circumstances. You don't really hurt yourself, for one thing, and you make sure there are people around to rescue you in time, for another. If Cornell had gone up on the roof and sat on the edge with his feet dangling over and shouted that he was going to jump, that would be a different thing. But to make a jump like that? No. Because you *might* get killed, jumping four stories onto the wooden roof of a storage shed, no matter if the shed is full of mattresses. And even if you don't get killed, you could get very severely injured. You could break bones, you could lose an eye. The sidewalk would be a cleaner and surer death, if you really mean to die, and the storage shed is too dangerous if you just want to call attention to yourself."

"But the police think it was suicide," she said.

"They won't for long. When Cornell comes to, he'll tell them what happened. With any luck, he knows who did it to him."

"What if he doesn't come to? What if he dies?"

"There are too many things obviously wrong with a suicide verdict," I said. "The fact that his partner was just killed a week and a half ago, in addition to everything else. They'll come around to murder."

"What if they don't?"

I shook my head. "Then I don't know," I said. "It won't be the first time anyone got away with murder in this city. But I don't think it'll happen."

"You won't do anything?"

"Me?" I frowned at her. "Why me?"

"He came to you for help," she said.

"And I helped him."

"And he sent you that beautiful scarf."

"Kate, he didn't buy me with that scarf. I didn't ask for it, he sent it as a thank-you for what I'd already done. He hasn't asked me to do anything else, and there's no need for me to do anything else. He's in a hospital now, the killer won't be able to get at him again, the police are on the job. If he comes to, he'll tell them what happened. If he doesn't, they'll investigate anyway."

"What if they don't?"

"It isn't my responsibility, Kate," I said.

She looked at me, and I could see her carefully not saying several different things. I am frequently amazed that she goes on putting up with me as I am now, and every time we come to a moment like this I feel a sudden pillar of cold in my chest, thinking, This is the time she leaves.

But it wasn't. She folded the paper, looking away from me, and in a neutral voice said, "Will you be working downstairs today?"

"Yes," I said.

"I'll be going shopping later on."

"All right."

She still hadn't looked at me. She got to her feet and carried the breakfast dishes over to the sink.

I wanted to say, *We know who I am, Kate, why be disappointed in it?* But I didn't say anything, and a little later I went down to the basement and went to work.

37

3

Three days later, Friday, they delivered the first load of building supplies for my sub-basement. Lengths of two-by-four, a bag of cement, two different sizes of concrete block; the bill was higher than I'd expected. It bothered me to write out the check, particularly when I was bringing no money into the house myself. This was Kate's money I was spending, more than mine, and though I knew she wouldn't grudge me, I didn't feel right about it.

The two men from the lumberyard weren't happy about delivering everything to the basement, but I worked with them and it didn't take that much time or effort. Then I paid them and they left, and I went back downstairs to go to work.

All I had done so far was dig. I had first used a sledge to break through the concrete floor in an area against the rear wall that extended ten feet along the wall and three feet out into the room. The broken pieces of concrete I had piled in a corner, after straightening the edges of the opened area as much as possible with a chisel and a smaller hammer. Then I'd started to dig, shoveling the dirt into empty cement bags, of which I had six. Whenever all six bags were full, I left off digging long enough to carry the bags one at a time upstairs and empty them in the back yard along the wall, the dark mounds looking odd surrounded by snow. All of this made for slow going, but that was, after all, the object.

I was digging a hole ten feet long and three feet wide, and I was digging steps in as I went, making the first step a long one because I would later cover these steps with the smaller concrete blocks. I had now dug to a depth of about four feet, and had four steps. I could begin at once to use some of the building supplies I'd bought.

From the beginning, I'd been digging wider than the opening I'd cleared in the floor, removing dirt from under both the exterior wall on the one side and the floor on the other. Now I began by building walls on both sides of my steps, one under the existing exterior wall and the other under the basement floor. I used concrete blocks, the larger ones, filled in crannies with smaller pieces of broken concrete from the pile in the corner, and used plenty of cement for mortar. I didn't want to finish with a wet cellar, nor did I want to weaken the structure of the house.

I did the walls as far as my fourth step, and was about to start laying the smaller concrete blocks on the steps and cementing them in place when Kate came down the stairs, slowly, looking thoughtful.

It was unusual for Kate to watch me at work, either down here or out in the yard when I was working on my wall. I glanced over at her and saw her sit down on the bottom step, watching me, her expression still distracted. I said, "Something?" and she shook her head, not as though there was nothing on her mind but as though she hadn't as yet worked out how to talk about it. I went on with my work.

I could feel her there, even though I didn't look directly at her, and it was a relief when, after about five minutes, she finally spoke, saying, "I went to the hospital today."

I straightened, a concrete block in my hands. Visions of incurable illnesses flashed through my head. More sharply than I'd intended, I said, "What's wrong? What's the matter?"

She smiled with sudden tenderness—I know she loves me, or why would she imprison herself here, but neither of us very often show our feelings—and said, "No, not about me. There's nothing wrong with me."

I felt stupid, standing there holding that heavy block. I half-turned to toss it onto the dirt bottom of the hole I was standing in, and said, "What, then?"

"I went to see Ronald Cornell," she said. "I called yesterday, and they said he was conscious and off the critical list. There wasn't anything in the paper about him today, so I went to see him."

There was going to be something in this I wouldn't like, or it wouldn't have taken her so long to get started. I said, "What did he have to say?"

"What you said. He didn't try to commit suicide. He was knocked out in the store, and didn't come to again until the hospital, day before yesterday."

"Did he see who did it?"

"No. He was in the back room of the store, sitting at his desk. He said he was doing some things with astrological charts. Whoever it was, they came up behind him. He didn't know anybody was in the store at all."

"It shouldn't take the police long to work it out," I said.

"That's the problem," she said. "The police aren't trying."

So here it was. I said, "What do you mean, they aren't trying?"

"They insist it was a suicide attempt," she said. "They're accusing Ronald of lying." Ronald. He had found a partisan, obviously.

I said, "That doesn't make any sense. They have to see he wouldn't do it that way."

"It seems mostly to be a detective named Manzoni. Did

you know him at all?"

"No. Cornell mentioned him when he was here. It was Manzoni that declared the Dearborn murder unsolvable."

"Well, he's the one saying Ronald tried to kill himself. Ronald says he's well known in the Brooklyn Heights area for hating homosexuals. He's been accused of beating them up two or three times."

That also did happen. A cop who hates a specific class or group of people—blacks, homosexuals, Jews, college students, union members, what-have-you—is in a better position than the average bigot to work out his hatred on individuals within that group. Generally, the force tries to avoid that kind of trouble by assigning men away from temptation— keeping the Negro-haters out of Harlem and Bedford-Stuyvesant, and the fag-haters out of Greenwich Village and Brooklyn Heights—but that kind of approach can't be one hundred percent effective. If Detective Manzoni actually did have a violent antipathy for homosexuals, he had been assigned to just the wrong part of the city; Brooklyn Heights has been a homosexual enclave for years.

I said, "In other words, Manzoni is blocking any real investigation."

"Yes. And there's nothing Ronald can do about it."

"He can go over Manzoni's head."

"Manzoni is trying to get Ronald committed to a mental institution. Because he tried to commit suicide, of course, and also because he's an admitted homosexual. Mitch, you know Manzoni won't have trouble finding some old-line judge to go along with him. And how can a certified lunatic complain to anybody and be listened to?"

"All right," I said. "He can't. But if you want *me* to go talk to Manzoni's superiors, believe me, I could only do more harm than good. I'm not the right kind of advocate for Cornell, what he needs is a good lawyer."

"Of course he needs a lawyer," she said. "But you know the kind of person he has for a lawyer. He's using the same lawyer he's always used in the past, for the store and whatever."

"You mean another homosexual."

"Yes. A man named Stewart Remington."

Stewart Remington? The name surprised me; it was one of the six I'd read to Eddie Schultz over the phone last week. So Cornell's lawyer was one of his suspects.

I said, "He should get another lawyer."

"I suppose he should. But he doesn't know how to tell Remington he wants somebody else, and he doesn't know any other lawyers."

"He's helpless, in other words."

Kate frowned at me. "You say that as though you think he's being a weakling or something. He really *is* helpless. He's in the hospital with half a dozen broken bones, there's a police guard on him, there's a detective with a vendetta against him, and he doesn't know what to do next. He *is* helpless."

"There's nothing for me to do," I said, because I knew that was the question behind all this: *Will you do something, Mitch?* "With my background," I said, "if I went to Manzoni's captain, it would just put the icing on the cake. Cornell would *really* be in the soup."

"He's really in the soup now."

"Well, what do you *want* from me?" I was getting exasperated. She clearly wanted something, she had it in mind there was something I could do, but she wouldn't come out and ask me. She just kept on describing Cornell's predicament. It was true that he was in deep trouble, but it was also true there was no sensible way I could help him.

So she said, "I want you to find the killer."

I couldn't believe it. "Are you out of your mind? Do you know what someone like Manzoni would do to me if he found me poking around, trying to open a case that he wants shut?"

"I hadn't expected an answer like that from you, Mitch. I expected you to say no at first, but not for that reason."

"I have my moments of bravery," I said, "like any other man. But I also have my moments of prudence. I don't see where this affair is any of my business. I want to stay away from it."

"It's a terrible miscarriage of justice," she said.

"Kate, there are terrible miscarriages of justice every day, in every city under the sun. There are three billion people on earth, and most of them will be treated shabbily and cruelly and even violently at least once in their lives. That isn't a *reason*, Kate, for me to stick my neck out."

"He needs your help, Mitch. He asked for your help. He has nobody else to turn to."

I could feel it closing in on me. "Kate, what on earth could I do? Even if I tried, what could I do? I can make some phone calls and find him a good lawyer, that would be the best thing."

"A lawyer won't beat Manzoni," she said, "not if Manzoni is determined. You know that, Mitch."

"Eventually—"

"Eventually? After a year, two years? Even six months, Mitch. Put someone like Ronald Cornell in an asylum for six months? What do you think it would do to him?"

I said, "There's no reason to believe I'd succeed, even if I did try."

"That's the worst excuse of all," she said.

I looked down at the hole I was digging, the concrete blocks I was putting in place. I didn't want to leave all this. I

didn't want to expose myself to anybody like Detective
Manzoni, I didn't want to pry into the unhappy world that
Ronald Cornell lived in, I didn't want to go out of this house
at all.

Kate said, "I talked to him about money."

I looked up at her in surprise. "Money?"

"He wouldn't want you to do it for nothing," she said.
"And we could use more money."

Neither of us looked directly at the new stacks of supplies
that had just been delivered, but all at once I was almost pain-
fully conscious of them, in the corner of my vision.

I said, "What kind of money were you talking about?"

"He told me his store has been averaging a profit of about
twenty thousand dollars a year, but they've been putting a lot
of it back into the business, for a wider stock and redecorating
the store and advertising and so on. So they don't have a lot of
money in cash. But now that his partner is dead, Ronald owns
the whole business outright, so he offered us a part owner-
ship. Fifteen percent."

"Fifteen percent of the store? For how long?"

"Forever. For as long as the store stays open. If the profit
keeps on the same as before, that's three thousand dollars a
year, every year. We could use something like that, Mitch."

Of course we could. Who couldn't use extra income every
year, with no work done for it?

Except at the beginning, of course. Work would have to be
done for it at the beginning.

I said, "To be paid to us if I find the killer?"

"No. Regardless of what happens, just if you'll agree to
try."

I shook my head. "I won't do it that way. If I don't succeed, I don't want any payment."

"Well, that would be up to you," she said, and from the

sudden lightening of her expression I saw that she had taken my last statement to mean that I was agreeing to take on the job.

And what else could I do? I remembered Ronald Cornell in this basement, timid and weak and ineffective, but pushing himself to be more, because his friend had been killed. Taking his coat and boots off before finding out if there was anyone at home or not, because he was determined to wait if the house was empty. It had to have been a strain for him to come to me, to come out of himself, to act. Just as it would be a strain for me.

Kate was saying, "I told the police I was his aunt, that's how they let me in. And I said his uncle might be coming to visit him, too."

"Did you see Manzoni at all?"

"No, and I'm glad I didn't."

"Does he have special visiting hours?"

"Yes. You could see him tonight, if you wanted, between seven-thirty and nine."

"All right," I said. "I'll go see him tonight."

"Thank you, Mitch," she said.

4

He looked like a cartoon in a magazine. He was as swathed in bandages as a mummy, and his right leg, in a hip-to-toe plaster cast, was held up at an angle by a system of weights and cords.

It was all a cartoon except the face. Lengths of adhesive tape over gauze were crisscrossed over his nose, but other than that, his head and face were clear of bandaging. The frightened, aching expression in his eyes could be read from across the room, and when he opened his mouth to talk—or to breathe—I could see that he was missing several teeth.

At first I thought the deep grayness around his eyes was the result of strain or tiredness, but then I realized he'd had two black eyes which were slowly fading. The result was to intensify his expression of pain and fear.

There was a uniformed policeman in a chair out in the hall, but Cornell and I were alone once inside the room. I walked over to the bed and said the usual inanity: "How are you?"

"Getting better," he said. He tried to smile at the same time, but his voice and his lips both quavered. He wasn't very far from tears.

He had the room to himself; the advantage of being under police guard. In addition to his bed and tray, there was a brown metal bureau against the opposite wall, a television set mounted on a high shelf across from the bed, a very large window covered with a shut venetian blind but no curtains or drapes, and two tubular chrome chairs with green plastic seats and backs, as though parts of a cheap kitchen set.

I had been surprised when I came in that he didn't have the television going, that boon to the bedridden, but now that I could see the screen, it turned out he *did* have it on, with the sound off. It was a black-and-white set, and the pictures were alternating close-ups of three earnest, intense, handsome and yet somehow artificial faces, one female and two male, apparently in intense discussion with one another. They looked real the way artificial limbs look real.

Cornell fumbled with a small black box in his right hand, and the television picture imploded in on itself and winked out. "Sit down," he said. "Thank you for coming." His voice was odd, different from what I'd remembered, more nasal and higher-pitched. That would be because of the bandages across his nose, of course; nature rarely does anything vicious to us without also, in the process, managing somehow to make us look foolish as well.

I pulled one of the chairs over by the bed. "My wife told me your situation," I said.

"It was very nice of her to come." She had been good for him, I could see that; his smile almost covered pain and fear completely.

I said, "Has anything else happened since she was here?"

"No. My lawyer is supposed to be here soon. Stewart Remington?"

"He was on the list," I said. "Your list of suspects."

He gave now a smile of helplessness; it covered nothing. "But I have to have a lawyer," he said. "What else am I going to do?"

"I know. Kate explained it to me."

"Mr. Tobin," he said earnestly, "I know your wife volunteered you to help me. I won't hold you to it against your will."

He was holding a door open for me, and in many ways it was a door I would gladly have gone through. But how could I, with Kate behind me, with Cornell's face in front of me? I said, "I'm not here against my will. It would have been easy for me not to come."

"I think you're a more private man than that," he said. "But I need you too much to offer twice. Thank you for coming."

I said, "Is your list of suspects still the same? No additions, no deletions?"

"It's still the same." He rested his head back on the pillow and gazed up at the blank television screen. "You know why I had the sound off when you came in? I was looking at those people talking, and they seemed so sure of themselves, so competent, so *able*. Whatever problem would face them, they would talk about it among themselves and *solve* it. Nothing would be too strong for them." He turned his head to smile sadly at me. "Do you know what I mean?"

"Yes."

He looked back at the screen again. "I was pretending they were talking about me. They were considering my situation, my past, my future, my personality. They were deciding what to do about me. All I had to do was lie here and wait, and they would come up with the decision. I didn't have to struggle any more, didn't have to think. They would decide, and act on the decision, and be very sure of themselves."

"I'm not them," I said.

The sad smile again. "You are to me."

"I need them, too. We all do."

"You are to me," he repeated. "That's why I gave you

the chance to walk away. Because I think you feel responsibilities very strongly."

"I'll just warn you now that I'm fallible, that the odds are not in my favor, that you may be disappointed."

He didn't say anything. He just smiled at me and shook his head. All at once I disliked him so intensely that I couldn't think of a word to say to him, none of the questions I wanted to ask, none of the suggestions I wanted to make. We just looked at one another, and his expression began to be uncertain, and the door behind me opened.

I saw my own relief mirrored in Cornell's eyes; the impasse interrupted. "Stew!" he called, and I got to my feet and turned around to take my first look at Stewart Remington, Cornell's lawyer.

Almost everything about him was a surprise. I'd expected someone more or less like Cornell, perhaps a bit brisker, more down-to-earth, but generally from the same mold. Stewart Remington, though, was from a different mold completely.

In the first place, he was about my age, around forty. And he was huge, over six feet by an inch or two, and fat the way pictures show Henry the Eighth was fat; a lot of flesh padding a large broad frame. I would guess him to be no less than three hundred pounds, and possibly ten or fifteen pounds over.

This huge body was draped in clothing which undoubtedly had come from Cornell's boutique. It was similar in style to what Cornell had worn the first time I'd seen him, but was more flamboyant in color and line. Looking at him, one knew he was the kind of man who wore a cape, and who wore one whether capes were in vogue that particular year or not, and who surely had at least one cape with a red satin lining.

What he was wearing now, however, was a black velvet

topcoat with black fur collar, the coat worn open, flung over his shoulders without his arms in the sleeves, like photos of Italian movie directors.

With all his size, and with all the flamboyance of his clothing, it was still his face which was his dominant feature. He had a large head, with masses of very curly thick black hair sweeping up and back and out above the fur collar. His forehead was broad and high and amazingly unlined, his eyebrows thick and black, his eyes piercing and deep-set and a very dark blue. He had a large lumpy formless nose, rather like W. C. Fields', but on Remington the effect was of imperial carelessness rather than comedy. His cheeks were very full, almost Santa Claus-like, but saved from that by the permanently sardonic expression of his broad and full-lipped mouth.

He had about him the look of the hedonist, the high-liver, the guzzler and the glutton and yet also the gourmet. He looked like the kind of man who would enjoy the best, but might enjoy it all too much. And when he took his hands from his jacket pockets I saw that he had rings on all his fingers, different styles and stones; they looked like the pudgy blunt-fingered hands of a silly rich widow, not like a man at all. The only sign of what he and Cornell had in common.

Cornell introduced us, and we shook hands; the soft hand, beringed, had no strength. All the strength was in Remington's eyes, as he studied me with a frankness much greater than the average.

Cornell said, "With you two on my side, I do have a chance."

Remington gave me a sardonic smile: one professional to another. "What do you think, Tobin? Will we save his pretty round butt for him?"

"Possibly," I said.

Remington laughed, a single boom, and said, "Confidence tempered with caution. The perfect note. Sit down, sit down, let's work out our fallen brother's salvation." He had the right voice to go with that kind of speech, a round baritone, loud without harshness. I wondered if he did much trial work, and if so, what sort of reaction his appearance and manner and voice got from the average jury.

We sat down, and Remington, overflowing the other tubular chair, said to me, "Have you met your opposite number yet?"

"Opposite number?"

"Manzoni, the scourge of the ungodly."

"No, I haven't."

"What a treat you have coming! A man blighted in his childhood by organized religion. After fifteen years surrounded by nuns, of *course* the rest of us look queer to him. Do you have influence anywhere on the force?"

"None."

"A pity," he said, and pursed his lips. He had shrugged his coat off his shoulders so that it hung backward now over the top of the chair, and he was sitting with his feet planted solidly on the floor, feet and knees spread wide apart as though he were prepared for the hospital to veer suddenly into heavy seas. Tucking his hands back into his side jacket pockets, he leaned against the back of the chair, and said, "That's what we need, you know. Someone from on high to sit with a great weight upon Manzoni's head. I'm doing all the expected legal waltz moves, but with the court calendars around this town, it takes six months to get permission to leave the room. By then, Manzoni can have our unfortunate friend committed, castrated, lobotomized and deported."

There was a question I had to ask, and there was no sense trying to find a roundabout diplomatic way to ask it, so I simply stated it direct: "Do you think it might help to bring in another lawyer?"

He closed one eye, glittered the other one at me, and smiled like the Cheshire Cat. "Someone's told you I sleep with boys," he said.

"That's part of it," I said.

"Happily," he said, "Detective Second Grade Aldo Manzoni may represent the Rheingold drinkers of our fair city, but once you get much above the level of the lip-readers, you'll find a fair degree of tolerance around and about. I expect I can do an attorney's job approximately as well as most heterosexual members of the Bar."

"I didn't mean that," I said. "I don't know what your regular field is—"

"The world is my regular field," he announced. He was prepared to be stern with me. We might both be working on the same task, but only one of us was going to be boss. "My practice has been varied," he said, and then winked broadly.

I was finding him tiresome. I said, "Cornell is satisfied anyway, and that's the main thing."

"Ronald's safety is the main thing," he corrected me. "And now, if we're finished studying *my* role in all this, would you mind terribly explaining yours? I had hoped Ronnie was presenting you as a man with some sort of clout on the police force."

Suddenly my job here seemed ridiculous. I described it in a monotone: "Cornell thinks his partner, Dearborn, was killed—"

"Dear Jamie. A loss. You never knew him, you'll have to take my word for it."

"Yes. Cornell thinks he was killed by someone he knew, some member of your circle. He was doing some investigating."

"Yes, he told me," Remington said. "And I found it very intriguing. Solving a murder astrologically. Has anyone ever done it before?"

"I wouldn't know," I said.

Cornell said, "Stew is interested, too. In astrology."

"More critically, perhaps, than some of the others in our little circle," Remington said, "but I do find it fascinating. And in this instance, of course, ultimately dangerous."

I said, "You don't doubt it was the same man who tried to kill Cornell."

"Not for a moment. Unfortunately, I am Remington and not Manzoni. Unfortunate in this instance only, I hasten to add."

"Cornell asked me to take over his investigation. If I turn up the guilty party, there won't be any more question of committing Cornell as an attempted suicide."

"Roundabout," Remington commented. "Be simpler to offer Manzoni a bribe, if he were bribable. Do you think he is?"

Cornell said, weakly, "I'm sure he isn't. I'm sure he wouldn't take a million dollars to lose the pleasure of doing me dirty."

Remington nodded judiciously. "My own estimate, exactly. But you yourself have been a policeman, have you not?"

"I have," I said. I wondered what he knew about me. I hoped it was no more than what he'd just said.

"When you see Manzoni," he went on, "do keep that in mind. If he looks to you as though he would prefer lucre to lunacy, see if you can find out how much it would take to turn him into a rational being."

I shook my head. "Even if he were the type to take it," I said, "which I doubt from what I've heard about him, I'm not the type to offer it. You'll have to do that yourself, if you want it done. And if you're going to do it, I'll have to bow out and have no more connection with the case."

Cornell said, anxiously, "No no, don't do that! I didn't say anything about a bribe, this is the first Stew's even mentioned it."

"I simply thought it would be quick and neat, if possible," Remington said, and shrugged his heavy shoulders expressively, to show he didn't much care one way or the other.

"If you decide to approach Manzoni that way," I said, "be sure to let me know first, so I can be well clear before you try it."

Remington smiled like a cupid. "When a man says something like that," he said, "I ask no more questions. Bribery is too dangerous to consider; consider it unconsidered."

"Good," I said, and saw that Cornell looked less anxious.

Remington said to me, "So what you're going to do is detect, is that it?"

"With any luck."

"Forgive me, but have you a license?"

"No."

"Now *you're* being frightening."

"Yes, I know," I said. "I can't apply for a license, for reasons of my own."

"I respect everyone's private reasons, and ask only for the same treatment in return. But what if the dread Manzoni turns his attention toward you? Can't he make life difficult?"

"If I'm not careful."

"So you intend to be careful." His smile this time was almost a smirk. "Most of my clients intended to be careful," he said. "But all of a sudden, there they were in Times Square with their trousers around their ankles. Very well, you'll be careful. In the meantime, is there anything I can do to be of assistance?"

"I think so," I said.

"You have only to ask."

"Good. The first thing I want to know is where you were at nine o'clock Monday evening."

His look of surprise may have been the first genuine un-amplified expression I'd yet seen from him, and it was short-lived, followed almost at once by a roar of laughter. Cornell was looking embarrassed, but neither of us paid him any attention. I sat there and watched Remington, and he rolled about, helpless with mirth, and watched me, and finally he allowed the tempest to subside; wiping tears of laughter from his eyes, he said, "So I'm on your little list, am I? That *will* complicate our teamwork, won't it? I was at the bath."

"All evening?"

"Oh, for hours and hours. I got there about seven, and I don't believe I left until well after three in the morning."

"I'm sorry," I said, "I don't follow you. You took a bath from—"

"No no, not *in* the bath, *at* the bath. The Borough Hall Baths, it's a public bath, maintained by the City of New York or the Borough of Brooklyn or some other excellent body. Swimming pool, steam rooms, massage, bathing, and lots of little cubicles with cots in which to"—he *did* smirk this time—"rest awhile. I love to go there." He turned and smirked at Cornell. "Ronnie used to go there, long long ago, didn't you, Ronnie?"

"Before Jamie." It was a whisper, but full of misery. Cornell had suddenly been given a vision of his future. Even without Detective Manzoni, it would be bleak.

I said, "Did anybody see you there, anybody who knew you?"

"Well, they *got* to know me, I do assure you of that. But honestly, you know, it's not exactly the sort of crowd that would like to get on a witness stand and say, 'Oh, yes, I was there and so was he.' It gets a little scary to talk about one's fun under oath like that."

"I'm not talking about oaths and courts," I said. "I'm talking about me."

"*I* know that. But would my witnesses? Tobin, I would love to clear myself off your list, but I can't think of a single person I could send you to who would admit to being at the bath himself, much less identify me as one of the other revelers there."

"All right. Let that go for a minute."

"Yes, let's."

"You said before that Cornell told you he was investigating Dearborn's murder. When did he tell you?"

"*After* the attempt on him, I'm happy to say. Right in this very room here. However, honesty compels me to admit I already knew it." Turning, grinning, to Cornell, he said, "You didn't exactly maintain tight security, Ronnie, you know. I imagine half a dozen people knew what you were up to. Jerry's the one who told me, and you know what a big-mouth Jerry is. What he knows, the whole world knows."

I said, "Who's Jerry?"

Remington looked back at me with a big happy beaming smile on his face. "My current darling," he said. "Just the sweetest little pudgy angel you've ever seen. All curves, no harsh angles."

Cornell, now embarrassed about me, said, "Stew, please!"

"You're right," Remington said, briskly but without remorse. "Jerry," he announced, as though it were the title of a speech he was about to make. "Jerry Weissman. Army brat. Nineteen years of age, currently sharing my bed and board.

56

Also a blabbermouth. Jerry Weissman."

I said to Cornell, "I don't remember that name from the list."

"He isn't on it," Cornell said.

"Why not?"

"He was with me the night Jamie was killed."

"With you?"

I thought I'd asked the question in a neutral way, but Cornell blushed and said, "Not like that. I wasn't—I never—"

"Ronnie and *Jamie* were lovers," Remington said, the sarcasm in his voice unsuccessfully hiding envy. "True to one another, with great exclusivity. A terrible waste, in my opinion."

I said to Cornell, "Where were you two?"

"In Atlanta," he said. "I come from there originally." My surprise must have shown, because he smiled faintly and said, "I know I don't sound like it. I worked very hard at that. And going to northern universities helped."

"But you were back in Atlanta the night Dearborn was killed? With—I'm sorry, I've forgotten the last name. Jerry . . ."

"Weissman," Remington said, rolling the name mock-lovingly off his tongue. "Just think of him as being beautifully white. Alabaster."

Cornell said, "Jerry's a designer, a men's fashion designer. He's just starting out, and we had him do some designs for us. There's a little place in Atlanta that makes up some of our things for us—"

"Cheap labor," Remington commented. "Non-union."

"That's exactly right," Cornell said, with something defensive in his tone. There were undercurrents between Cornell and Remington on this point, but I couldn't tell what they were. Cornell went on, "We flew down Saturday

morning, Jerry and I, talked to the people there in the afternoon, and stayed over Saturday night. We flew back Sunday.
That's when I found . . ." Instead of finishing the sentence,
Cornell shook his head and moved his hands vaguely in the
air.

"All right," I said. "Do you have anything written down
from your investigations? Lists of names, alibis, anything like
that?"

"It's all in my desk at the shop," he said. "At least, it was. I
don't know, maybe he did something with it all after he hit
me."

"Nobody's checked?"

"I didn't ask anybody to. Jerry might know, he's been
keeping the shop running this week. We can't afford to stay
closed any longer."

"Then he's the one I should see for the keys." To
Remington, I said, "At your place?"

"Sadly, no," he said, and Cornell explained, "Jerry's
staying at my apartment. There has to be someone there for
the cats, and so the place doesn't get robbed."

"Does he know about me? Can I go to see him directly?"

"I told him about you," Cornell said. "He doesn't know
yet that you're going to help, but he knows who you are."

"Then I'll go see him," I said, and got to my feet. "I'll
probably come back and talk to you again tomorrow."

Remington didn't stand. He said, "I'm in the book,
Tobin, if you need me for anything except alibis. The
Brooklyn book. And you?"

"Queens," I said. "Under my wife's name. Katherine
Tobin."

Cornell said, "I appreciate this, Mr. Tobin."

I was about to point out that I hadn't yet done anything for
him to appreciate, but of course I had. His spirits were

improved, at least temporarily. I said, "I'll see you later."

From the door, I looked back and saw them both watching me, Cornell's eyes full of hope and pleading, Remington's expression sardonic. Remington had one glittering hand resting on the bed, near Cornell's elbow. Cornell's leg jutted up at an angle in its cast.

I knew that Remington would not talk against me behind my back, and yet I felt that he would. I closed the door, nodded to the bored cop in the chair in the hall, and left.

5

There are a few picturesque corners of New York City, contrasting with the city's general drabness, and of these one of the prettiest is Brooklyn Heights. A little section of narrow streets, trees and brownstones, it has a quiet and dignified appearance, and from parts of it can be seen a beautiful view of the skyscrapers of lower Manhattan, across the waters of the mouth of the East River. The actual waterfront is given over to piers and warehouses, as usual in New York, but on the heights above the waterfront there is a highway, the Brooklyn-Queens Expressway, which for this part of its length is roofed over, the roof forming the Brooklyn Heights Promenade, a narrow parklike walk with trees and benches and a wide-ranging view of New York Harbor, from Brooklyn Bridge on the right to Governor's Island and Buttermilk Channel on the left. The Promenade has become a habitual locale for cruising homosexuals out to meet new friends, and every once in a while is the scene of a late-night mugging. But neither apes nor perverts detract much from the charm and beauty of the area.

It was in the middle of the best part of Brooklyn Heights that Ronald Cornell lived, not two blocks from the Promenade. I had trouble finding a parking space, which is standard for that section, and had to walk back three blocks. There had been more snow in the last week, and only a narrow meandering path had been cleared along most of the sidewalks.

Cornell's house was a brownstone, fairly wide, four stories tall, with its high front stoop intact. And carefully cleared of snow, as was the full width of sidewalk across the building front. I went up the steps, stamping snow off my shoes, and pushed open the tall narrow glass-paneled door into the tiny foyer.

The building was divided into two apartments, one taking the floor at this level and the floor below, the other on the top two floors. Since I understood that Cornell owned this building, I was surprised to see the card "Dearborn-Cornell" next to the upper bell button. I pushed, and a moment later there was a buzzing, and I went through the front doorway into a hall dominated by red flocked wallpaper and rich Persian carpeting. The carpeting continued up the staircase, which filled most of the hall space; just out of sight at the head of the stairs a door opened, causing light-spill to accentuate even more the dramatic wallpaper.

The bordello effect would have been Dearborn's idea; it wasn't Cornell's style.

A blond head appeared up there: "Here we are! Come on up!"

I went on up, and as I approached I got a better look at the blond head. Was this Jerry Weissman? From what Cornell—and Remington—had said, I'd expected something other than this.

He was tall and willowy, with the seamless smiling face of the innocently depraved. The blond hair was not quite the right blond to be real, and considering the season, his deep tan looked equally artificial. He made me think of surfers and teen-age beach movies. He was the younger brother—and practically the younger sister—of the simulated human beings Cornell had been watching on television. He was dressed in white slacks and a pale blue pullover shirt, and was barefoot.

Could this be Jerry Weissman? I asked the name, half-expecting him to say no, and then had all my preconceptions twisted out of my reach when he *did* say no. "I'm Cary Lane," he said, smiling at me, showing me teeth that didn't look in any way real. "And if you aren't Mitch Tobin, I don't know *why* I let you in."

"I am Mitch Tobin."

"I just knew it! You have a look of quiet strength." And I had the uncomfortable feeling he was about to stroke my cheek. But he didn't; instead, he stepped back and made a welcoming gesture, saying, "Come on in, Mitch, Jerry's inside. Oh! Watch the cat!"

An all-white cat had abruptly snaked through his white-clad legs, grimly intent on reaching the stairs. I bent with a quick scooping motion, was lucky enough to grab the cat in time, and walked into the apartment holding the animal in my arms. It had gone limp at once, and when Cary Lane shut the door I let the cat drop again, and it walked off as though it had never wanted to leave at all.

"Very nicely done," Lane said admiringly. He made a willowy little hand motion, as though drying nail polish, to gesture me to go to the right. "Jerry's in there," he said.

I was remembering that Cary Lane was one of the names on Cornell's list. "Thank you," I said, and turned right.

New York City apartments frequently are laid out very awkwardly, the result of being adaptations from the original intent of the building. This building, for instance, would have been at the time of its construction around the turn of the century a private home, with kitchen and servant's quarters on the ground floor, living and dining rooms on the second, and bedrooms and baths on the third and fourth. The alteration to a pair of independent apartments had left some anomalies, among them the entrance to the upper apartment.

The entrance was to a blank wall, the top of the stairs having emerged midway along a corridor running from front to back. To the left along that corridor was what looked like an unusually large kitchen for New York, and to the right—the direction Lane had steered me—was the living room.

The Dearborn aura continued dominant. The corridor had been lined on both sides with posters, both old ones of movies and circuses and new ones of art shows and rock groups, and now the living room was full of inflatable plastic furniture, lucite tables, strange light fixtures and oddly placed fur throws. There were two windows facing the street, curtainless; the white shades were pulled all the way down, and large stylized eyes had been drawn on them, one each. The one on the left was open, the one on the right was shut.

I automatically looked to my left, at the wall those windows faced, to see what they were staring (winking? glaring?) at, and saw the entire wall spread with a huge color photograph of a Boeing 747 in flight, coming directly this way.

Behind me, Cary Lane giggled and said, "*Everybody* does that! Everybody looks!"

"I suppose they do," I said, but I was looking now at the other two young men in the room and realizing that the smell in the air was marijuana.

Which of these would be Jerry Weissman? But it was easy to tell, really. The very young one, no more than twenty, in sneakers and blue jeans and T-shirt; he would be Jerry Weissman. He had an ordinary youthful face, set in an expression of slightly anxious eagerness to please. He was of average height but a bit chunky, with a soft layer of baby-fat that made him look somewhat clumsy, though when he got up from the clear plastic inflated armchair—which I later found it difficult to get out of—he moved with the automatic grace of an athlete.

His voice too was young and soft, like his face and body: "Mr. Tobin. Ronnie said you might come over. I'm Jerry Weissman." And he extended his hand toward me.

I was surprised at the strength of his handshake. It went more with the eagerness of his expression than with his general appearance. "Cornell told me you might be able to help," I said.

"If I can," he said earnestly. "I guess you met Cary already. This is David Poumon."

"How do you do?"

David Poumon had been standing already when I'd come into the room, leaning against the white wall-space between the windows, frowning thoughtfully at the 747. He seemed older than both Weissman and Lane, but in a strange way. It wasn't as though many years separated him from them, he was probably no older than Lane, but as though a full generation had somehow elapsed in his life that had not as yet elapsed in theirs.

He had thinning black hair, brushed straight back across a neat small round skull. He wore large glasses with round metal frames, behind which his face seemed slightly shriveled and very pale. A brooding kind of intelligence flickered like St. Elmo's fire over that face, and I noticed that he seemed to blink much less often than most people. He was wearing ordinary slacks, very like casual slacks back home in my own closet, and a white shirt with the sleeves rolled up above the elbows. Black loafers and black socks were on his feet. When we shook hands, it was like holding a rubber bag full of bones; not strong, but not soft either.

"Sit down, Mr. Tobin," Jerry Weissman said. "Do you want coffee? Something to drink?"

None of them were smoking now, and I wondered if they'd stubbed out the marijuana cigarette in honor of my appearance here. I didn't see it in any of the ashtrays, so I couldn't tell how short the butt was.

I said, "Nothing, thank you. I just want to talk."

"There's coffee already made," Weissman assured me. "Sit down here, I'll go get some. I want some anyway, it won't take a minute. Here, sit down."

He was obviously the kind of person who can't think about anything else until they've had the chance to fulfill some sort of self-imposed requirement as host. It was easier to give in, so I agreed to coffee and settled myself in the bulgy inflated plastic armchair he'd just gotten out of. It was surprisingly comfortable, but a little too lively.

Weissman hurried from the room, continuing to cast assurances over his shoulder that this wouldn't take but a minute, and I was left with Cary Lane and David Poumon. I looked at them with interest, because both names had been on Cornell's list.

Poumon had backed into the wall again and returned to his original stance, from which he was now broodingly surveying me instead of the 747. Lane had arranged himself like Jean Harlow on a couple of fur throws on the floor, and was smiling at me with open-hearted happiness.

I said, "Did you believe Cornell about what had happened to Jamie Dearborn? Before Monday, I mean."

"Oh, *I* did," Lane said promptly. "I can't think of anything that man Manzoni could possibly say that wouldn't be wrong."

Poumon, more soberly, said, "It seemed to me the police theory didn't take Jamie's personality into account."

"Imagine Jamie picking up rough trade!" Lane announced. "Oh, my *dear*, it isn't within the *realm*."

"Did you know Cornell was trying to find the murderer?"

"Wasn't that exciting?" Lane clasped his hands under his

chin and made his shoulders shiver. "He told us all about it. We were on his suspect list and everything!"

"When did he tell you?"

"Oh, ages ago."

Poumon, smiling thinly to show he'd understood the purpose of the question, said, "Before the attempt on his life."

"Oh, long before that," Lane said, still oblivious. "Days and days and days." Suddenly he sat straighter and pointed a dramatic finger at me. "And now," he declaimed, "it's *your* turn. The investigation goes on!" He beamed with pleasure.

Poumon said, "I suppose you'd like to know where Cary and I were Monday night."

Lane looked baffled. "Good heavens, why?"

Poumon gave him a surprisingly tender smile. "Because, bubblehead, we're *still* on the suspect list."

"Oh, mercy, of course!" He laughed, delighted to be on the list. "Mitch," he said, leaning toward me, "can't you just see me? *Sneaking* up behind poor unsuspecting Ronnie, *bashing* him a good one with something terribly suggestive and phallic, then *lugging* him up all those stairs. Would I kiss him good-bye, do you suppose? Before the old heave-ho?"

"Would you?" I asked him.

Lane laughed again, and then began to look a little uncertain. "You aren't having fun, Mitch," he said.

Poumon told him, "He isn't playing the game, Cary. He's very serious."

"Seriousness makes me nervous," Lane said. Sitting up straight, he bent his knees, wrapped his arms around his legs, rested his chin on his knees, and looked reproachfully at me. "I never know how to act when people are serious," he said, pouting a bit. "Like Stew." And then, precisely like Stewart Remington, "Cary, you *must* shape up." Because his chin remained stationary on his knees when he talked, his head

66

bobbed with every word; it was strange to hear Remington's baritone coming out of that bobbing blond head.

He needed to be smiled at, to be told that nothing was serious after all, the way most people need to breathe. He was good at wheedling that sort of response, obviously; the smile I gave him now was small and grudging, but honest, and he smiled back at once, managing to smile through tears without actually having shed any tears.

Weissman came back with a tray loaded with coffee cups and saucers, spoons, sugar, cream and an electric coffee-maker. There was a certain amount of confusion now as he set the tray on the floor between Poumon and me and distributed coffee around to everyone.

I could no longer smell the marijuana, and I suspected they hadn't smoked much of it before I'd arrived. I know the popular conception of marijuana seriously overrates its powers but, like alcohol, it does begin to show an effect, and these young men might have had no more than a couple of drinks. Lane was being somewhat odd and flamboyant, but I imagined that was his style most of the time.

When we finally got our coffee, and Weissman settled on another inflated chair, I spent a few seconds trying to think how best to bring the conversation back to Monday night. Before I formulated my next question, though, Poumon did it for me, saying, "About our alibis for Monday. Unfortunately, neither of us has one."

"Well, *I* know where I was," Lane said. He acted miffed.

"But nobody else knows you were there," Poumon pointed out.

"Where?" I asked.

"The ballet," Lane said. He raised his arms over his head and pretended a pirouette. "I love the ballet."

"You went alone?"

"I always go alone. David won't come with me"—with a little pout in Poumon's direction—"and I'm disgustingly faithful. Besides, the ballet is so intensely *personal* an experience, at least I think so."

I said, "What about your seat? The ballet's all subscription, isn't it? We could find the people in the seats on both sides of yours, and they'd surely remember whether your seat was occupied or not."

"Oh, no," he said. "I couldn't go like that. So *structured*."

"I don't follow you."

"If I *feel* like going to the ballet," he said, "I just *go*."

Poumon explained, "There's almost always a few people selling their subscription seats outside the door. Cary just goes and buys a ticket."

"I almost never fail to get a seat," Lane said happily.

So that was no good. Lane wouldn't be the type to keep his stubs, nor to remember exactly where he sat. And if he was as much a ballet buff as he sounded, he would not only know which ballets were performed last Monday (whether he'd actually been there or not), but would surely have seen them several times in the past.

I turned to Poumon. "And you?"

"At home," he said. "Alone, with Cary out. Working."

"You'd *better* be alone," Lane told him, with mock ferocity.

I said, "Working? At what?"

"Music," he said. "I'm learning to be a composer."

"And you have no way to prove you were really home all evening."

"I'm sorry, no."

"Neither do I," Jerry Weissman said. "Am I a suspect?"

"I understand you were in Atlanta with Cornell when Dearborn was killed."

"That's right, I was. So that clears me, doesn't it?"

"Yes. Cornell tells me you've been keeping the store running this week."

"As much as I could," he said. His unassuming modesty didn't ring quite true; I thought he was probably very proud of himself for having been such a good Samaritan. Self-congratulation lurked just beneath the surface of his modest smile.

"Could you let me in there this evening?"

"Surely. No trouble at all."

The color photograph of the 747 was beginning to get to me. It showed nothing but sky and clouds and that huge fat plane. There was nothing solid, nothing to anchor oneself to. The room, with that picture dominating it, with the other walls so totally white (except for the eyes on the window shades), and with all this transparent furniture, gave an atmosphere of spaciousness and floating, but not in a good way. I was almost getting airsick in here, the effect was one of disorientation. I said, "Is this the room where Dearborn was killed?"

"No. That was upstairs. Do you want to see it?"

"Yes."

I managed to get up from the chair, and put my coffee cup on a nearby transparent lucite cube table. "This way," Jerry Weissman said.

Between the corridor doorway and the far wall, there was just space for another door, painted completely white, even the knob. Weissman opened this door, and a rather narrow flight of stairs led upward. I motioned for him to go first, which he did reluctantly, and I followed. Poumon and Lane stayed behind in the living room.

The interior walls had been removed on the top floor, which had been turned into a giant bedroom, twenty feet wide and fifty feet long. Only this staircase, some wide closets and a smallish bathroom shared the space up here.

And again it was Dearborn's taste—or at least I assumed so—that predominated. The long wall opposite the staircase was papered in bold tiger stripes, and the entire ceiling was painted a flat black, so that it virtually disappeared. Both ends of the room were almost totally windows, those in front translucent and those in back of clear glass, and now I could see why Cornell had chosen the top apartment rather than the bottom. The view out the back, over the tops of a few smaller buildings, was of the Manhattan skyline; just about the same view as from the Promenade, but four stories higher. At night like this, with the black ceiling and the dark maroon carpet keeping the room unobtrusive, the strings of lights that were the Manhattan skyscrapers and the necklace of lights that was the Brooklyn Bridge were unbelievably impressive. It was the most beautiful view of New York I'd ever seen.

"None of us had ever seen this place," Jerry Weissman said. "Isn't it something?"

"It certainly is. You never saw it before now?"

"Ronnie and Jamie kept the top floor just for themselves. Guests had to stay downstairs. They made a whole thing about it, you know? Their private world."

"A beautiful world," I said.

Weissman pointed beyond the bed. "He was found on the floor over here."

I looked at him. I wanted to ask someone how any human being could commit murder in front of these windows, but Jerry Weissman wasn't the one to ask.

Perhaps I would get a chance to ask the murderer.

I didn't want to see any more. I didn't want to see where Jamie Dearborn was found dead. I didn't want to walk around in anybody else's private world. "Let's go to the shop," I said.

Weissman looked surprised, but made no comment. "Of course," he said. "It's just a couple blocks, we can walk it."

I went first back down the stairs.

6

David Poumon and Cary Lane walked a block with us. They lived in the neighborhood, and were going home.

After they left us, I said to Weissman, "Tell me about those two."

He said, "You don't really think they did it, do you? Either one of them?"

"I don't know yet. Tell me about them."

"I don't know what to tell," he said. "Cary's from Los Angeles originally. He's a model."

"Like Jamie?"

"Yes, with the same agency."

"Any jealousy between them?"

"Oh, Lord, no. You saw Cary, he doesn't worry about anything like that. He bought that face and he's absolutely happy with it. He isn't jealous of anybody."

"He bought the face? How do you mean?"

"Plastic surgery," Weissman said casually, as though that were all the explanation I would need.

"Was he in an accident?"

"No, nothing like that. He just didn't like the way he looked, he thought he was too ordinary." He grinned unselfconsciously and said, "I suppose he used to look something like me. So he did himself all over, top to bottom."

"The face is completely new?"

"I don't know what he looked like before; he says he's

72

destroyed all the old pictures, even some his mother tried to hide. But I guess it's all brand-new, yes."

"And the hair? That didn't look real."

"Oh, Lord, no, that's straight out of the bottle."

"And the teeth?"

"Caps, all across the front."

I said, "He didn't change his height, did he?"

Weissman laughed and shook his head. "No, he's the same height. We turn here." We turned, and he said, "But he lost weight. Apparently he used to be kind of fat, like me."

Weissman wasn't fat. He had a layer of baby-fat over a somewhat chunky frame, but he wasn't fat.

They made a nice study in contrasts, Weissman constantly diminishing himself, making himself a servant, denigrating his appearance, and Cary Lane exalting himself from within an entirely manufactured frame. I said, "Is that his real name? Cary Lane?"

"Yeah, it is, isn't that weird? People in California have names like that, I don't know why."

"How old is he?"

"I think Cary's twenty-eight now."

A good six years older than I would have given him. I said, "And the other one? Poumon?"

"Dave's twenty-four."

And I had been thinking of Poumon as the older; a generation older. I said, "Tell me about him. Poumon."

"He's from Canada. Toronto. He wants to be a composer."

"So he said. Serious music, or popular?"

"That's hard to say these days, isn't it?" Weissman said, and nodded ahead of us. "Here we are."

Jammer had begun life as an ordinary storefront in a building that had apartments above; the kind of storefront in

73

which to find barbershops or tailors. There had originally been two display windows, with a recessed entrance in the middle, a perfectly ordinary design.

It was ordinary no longer. The display windows had been covered with sheets of plywood painted a garish bright pink. Four-foot-tall letters, also cut from plywood and painted an equally bright purple, stood out three inches or so from the pink plywood, spelling JAMMER, three letters on each side of the entrance. The two M's were narrower than the other letters, cramped-looking, as though the entrance had been forced between them as an afterthought. And the entrance itself was a completely plain black door with a single glass porthole in it at eye-level and a brass letter-slot at about the level of my waist.

I stood to one side while Weissman unlocked the door and reached inside to switch on some lights, and then we both went in.

Inside, it was very crowded and disorganized-looking, with round racks of clothing everywhere, counters on both sides, shelves up behind them, and narrow meandering aisles for customers amid the confusion of stock. The ceiling, a mass of heat ducts, exposed wiring, suspended fluorescent lights, plumbing and odd angles, had been painted flat black —like the top-floor ceiling in Cornell's apartment—undoubtedly in order to get rid of it.

Weissman said, "I guess you want to see the office. It's back here."

I followed him—with the bright colors and the crowding, it was more like being in a plastic jungle than a clothing store —and at the rear we went around a counter piled with see-through shirts, through a hanging paisley drape, and directly into the nineteenth century.

It was an office out of Dickens: small, piled high with

papers, crowded with old furniture made of wood. There was no paint on any of the wood, only stain that let the grain show through. There was a very old roll-top desk, a wooden swivel chair, even a tall wooden filing cabinet. The calendar on the wall above the desk was of this new year we had just embarked on, but the picture was a Currier & Ives print of ice-skaters, and the company which had sent out the calendar—a belt and wallet maker in Philadelphia—had chosen an old-fashioned kind of script for its name and message.

Was I at last in the influence of Ronald Cornell? All the rest of it, the apartment, the storefront, the store itself, seemed to bear the heavy stamp of Jamie Dearborn, whose confident Now face I had seen only once in the advertisement Cornell had shown me. But this room was not Dearborn; Dearborn would have made it all Camp somehow, would have mocked the spirit of wood. This was no fey imitation of a bygone style, it was a room that a man worked in, and which he had made comfortable for himself so he could do his work better.

I said to Weissman, "Did Cornell do most of the business details around here?"

"Oh, sure," he said. "Jamie brought in the customers, you know, he was the contact man. But Ronnie did all the paper-work." He looked around the little office, smiling. "Jamie hated this place. He kept threatening he was going to come in some day and rip it all out and turn the place into a big white cube. Translucent white glass on all the walls and the floor and the ceiling, with fluorescent lights behind them. And two more white cubes in the middle of the floor, one with a type-writer on it and the other for Ronnie to sit on."

"Did he mean it?" I asked. It occurred to me that men had killed other men for less violent forms of rape.

"No, not really. He meant he thought it would be better

that way, look better, but it would, wouldn't it? Ronnie likes all this old stuff, though, so Jamie wouldn't actually *do* anything to it."

I thought of Ronald Cornell in the living room we'd just left, with the 747 perpetually in flight, perpetually coming at him. I thought of the clothing he'd worn when he'd come to see me. I was beginning to understand just how totally he'd submerged himself within a reflection of Jamie Dearborn, and just how empty he must be now, with Dearborn gone. Cary Lane had gone ahead and superimposed his ideal onto his own body, but Cornell had sought it in another person and then lived on reflected light, like the moon with the sun.

I sat down at the desk, and Jerry Weissman stood back and watched me, attentive, prepared at any time to be of assistance. The top was shut, and I tried it experimentally, to find it wasn't locked. I rolled it back, and the surface of the desk—like the top, like the top of the filing cabinet, like the surface of the small wooden table against the opposite wall, like the floor beside the desk—was spread with a thick confusion of papers. I began to poke through them, and saw at once that the confusion was more apparent than real. The papers to the right had to do with the business of the store, but the papers to the left had to do with the killing of Jamie Dearborn.

That they were still here disappointed me, to some extent. I had no doubt the killer had sat here last Monday evening, as I was doing now, and had gone very carefully through these papers. That he hadn't taken them with him, or destroyed them, meant he felt there was nothing dangerous in them, nothing that would lead anyone to him.

Unless he had been selective, had only removed one or two sheets? I would eventually bring the whole pile to Cornell at the hospital, and he could see if anything was missing.

For the moment I just glanced quickly through all the

papers, sorting out those that had to do with the murder. About half of them seemed to have some bearing on astrology, and I considered leaving these behind, but eventually decided to include them, too. Four books on astrology were also on the desk, up amid the secondary confusion on top, but I didn't take them. I leafed through them for any papers or notes they might contain, found nothing, and returned them to their places.

The desk drawers produced nothing of value to me except a large manila envelope in which to carry the papers I wanted, which made up a pile about an inch thick. I put the papers in the envelope, finished my search of the desk, got up to check out the filing cabinet, found nothing of interest there, and turned back to Jerry Weissman: "Now the stairs," I said.

"Sure. This way."

We went back out to the store proper, and immediately turned left, going along behind the counter with the see-through shirts, and then left again through another paisley drape, this time to a strictly functional rear staircase, which had obviously been left in its original condition. I became aware again of how totally Jammer had created its own environment within the building, so that the store and the rest of the building no longer had any sort of common bond at all.

The stairs were very narrow, and seemed to have been put on the rear of the building as an afterthought. They doubled back on themselves halfway up each floor, and at these landings there were windows that looked out on, presumably, some sort of back yard. Only darkness could be seen out there now. Green wooden doors were closed at each story, facing other windows; at the third floor there was a bag of clothespins hanging on the wall beside the window. I heard nothing from within any of the apartments we passed.

The final flight led to a trapdoor, fastened on the inside by a large nail stuck through the ring of a hasp lock. Weissman removed this nail, set it to one side on a step, pushed up on the trapdoor, and we went on up the stairs to the roof.

And here was another reason for the killer to push Cornell off the back rather than the front. The rear edge of the roof was no more than three feet from the trapdoor. It must have been tiring work to drag Cornell's body up four flights of stairs, and a strong temptation to simply roll him off the nearest edge at the top.

And without leaving any sign. I had hoped for useful marks in the snow on the roof, but there were none. Of course, there had been more snow since Monday, and wind. I wondered if anything useful might have been found that first night, had the police been in a mood to look.

"All right," I said. "Let's go back down." It seemed colder up here than it had before in the street.

We went back down the wooden stairs. The light was poor, low-wattage bare bulbs in the ceiling at each floor, but even with floodlights I knew I would find no signs of the murderer's passage, not four days after the event

At the first floor, instead of a window facing out back, there was another green door, this one securely fastened with a padlock. I said, "Is the storage shed through there?"

"Yes. You want to see it?"

"Please."

Weissman produced his key ring again, and unlocked the door. "The light isn't working," he said. "Just a second." He fumbled around inside, and produced a long flashlight. "Here we are," he said, and switched it on.

The shed was as I'd imagined it: simple, wooden, unheated, with a concrete floor. Soft-drink cases had been placed face down on this floor and one-by-twelves stretched across them. On these were stored the bolts of cloth, as brightly colored and fantastically designed as anything in the shop itself.

Weissman said, "Some of the cloth was ruined, of course. Stew's trying to see if we can collect on the insurance." He flashed the light upward, and I saw the hole where Cornell had crashed through. He had torn down the light fixture with his passage, and had left a ragged, jagged hole oddly circular in shape, about three feet in diameter. Boards had been laid across the roof to cover the hole and protect the interior from the elements. "We'll have to get it fixed soon," Weissman said. "If there's a thaw, that stuff I put up there won't keep the water out. But we can't do anything until we hear from the insurance company."

"Why is the cloth here?" I asked. "Do you make the stuff you sell?"

"Not really. But lately a lot of men"—he used the term without apparent self-consciousness—"have gotten into doing their own clothes. So we sell material, too. And patterns. I do some patterns, and then you can get some commercially, too. Not much yet, but it's coming in."

"I see. You aren't a partner, are you?"

"Oh, Lord, no. I get a percentage on patterns they sell, naturally. And when they sell things that were made from my designs, I get a part of that, too. Also, I help out in the store sometimes, I clerk and like that, and Ronnie pays me."

"What about Stewart Remington? I understand you live with him?"

He suddenly blushed, and seemed very flustered. "Well, sort of. Just for a while, you know, until I get used to New York. I haven't been here very long."

Weissman wasn't a suspect; I wasn't interested in him. I said, "Remington is Cornell's lawyer. Did he do the legal work for the store?"

"Oh, of course. He does all our legal work, the whole crowd. Whatever we might need, contracts or whatever. And he does our taxes, and he's Jammer's accountant." He smiled, over his embarrassment now. "He's sort of our link to the square world," he said. "He makes sure we have all our i's dotted."

I would have to talk with Remington again, away from Cornell. I stepped back out of the storage shed, saying, "What about Bruce Maundy?"

"Bruce?" Weissman shut the door and put the padlock back in place. "He's all right. He wants to be a playwright. Actually, he's had a couple of things produced. In coffee houses, you know. Off-Off-Broadway."

We went back into Jammer. I said, "Does he live around here, too?"

"No, in Queens. He lives at home with his mother."

"Does he do anything for a living? Besides the play-writing."

"Oh, sure. He works for a ticket agency in Manhattan. To be near the theater, you know." Weissman grinned, poking amiable fun at his friend's pretensions.

I remembered the other two names from Cornell's suspect list. "Leo Ross," I said. "Tell me about him."

"He's an interior decorator, he and Henry Koberberg have a business together. I understand they're very successful."

Henry Koberberg was the final name on the list. "Do they live together?"

"Yes."

"Around here?"

"They used to, but they moved to Manhattan last year. Before I came around. I never saw their old place. The new place is really beautiful, it's like being inside a giant plant."

"Where in Manhattan?"

"In the East Sixties."

A very expensive section; Leo Ross and Henry Koberberg must be doing very well indeed. I said, "And is Remington their lawyer, too?"

"Oh, sure. He takes care of all of us."

I wondered if Weissman's strong sense of community was shared to that degree by the others. Lane and Poumon both seemed, in their varying ways, too self-centered for that. I remembered Remington's description of Weissman as an "Army brat," by which I inferred that Jerry Weissman was the son of a professional career Army man. If that was true, Weissman had undoubtedly grown up in a dozen or more different locales around the world, depending on his father's shifting assignments. That would tend to produce the strong desire for a feeling of community that Weissman was displaying.

But Weissman was not on the list. There were six others I had to concern myself with. I said, "I'd like to see these people, but I wish it could be casual some way."

"There's going to be a party at our place tomorrow night," Weissman said. "Why don't you come?"

"Your place?"

"You know, Stew's place. Stew Remington. Most Saturdays there's a party at one place or another, and it's kind of our turn tomorrow night."

"I'd be glad to come," I said.

A frown touched his face, a sudden doubt. He said, "There won't be any straight people there, you know."

"If it's a party," I said, "and not an orgy, I'll be happy to be there."

"Oh, no, just a party. People might go off into another room after a while, something like that, but it won't be, you know, a lot of naked carrying-on or anything like that."

"Then I'll come."

"Fine," he said, and gave me a sunny smile, and I realized his wide-ranging net had just included me within his community.

7

Henry Koberberg
Cary Lane
Bruce Maundy
David Poumon
Stewart Remington
Leo Ross

It was a mark of Cornell's character that he would bother to make his list of suspects in alphabetic order.

I stayed up late Friday night, studying the papers I had taken from his desk at Jammer. His pre-astrology steps had been careful and reasonable and perfectly competent detective work. Under the heading "People Jamie would have let into the apartment," there appeared a list of fourteen names; his starting point. And why not? Even if Dearborn had buzzed to let the murderer in the front door before looking to see who it was—and all he had to do was come to the head of the stairs and look down and through the glass of the door to identify the caller—the killer still had to go up that flight of stairs and through another door. And there had been no indication of forced entry; Jamie Dearborn had agreed to the entrance of his murderer into his home.

Cornell knew his friend, I had to accept that. If in his judgment Dearborn would not have permitted anyone other than these fourteen people into the apartment, there was no reason for me not to go along with him.

Gradually, Cornell had whittled the fourteen names to six, and his reasons for eliminating each suspect were methodically written out in detail, a separate sheet of paper for each name. But finally he had come to the point where he could reduce the list by logic and factual research no further, and it was at this point he had turned to astrology.

In many ways, the papers relating to his astrologic search were the most fascinating of all, and in addition to what I looked upon as astral mumbo-jumbo, they also gave me many facts about the suspects I hadn't known before: the age of each, for instance, and the place of birth.

And Jamie Dearborn's place of birth, as well, Cornell having cast his friend's horoscope in apparent hopes of finding something in it that would connect to the horoscopes of one of the suspects. I had assumed Dearborn to be a New Yorker, or at least an Easterner, but it turned out he had been born in Omaha, Nebraska. Which undoubtedly explained why there were no relatives of his among the fourteen names on Cornell's original list.

Of the six remaining suspects, three were born New Yorkers: Henry Koberberg, born thirty-six years ago in Manhattan; Bruce Maundy, twenty-six years ago in Queens; and Stewart Remington, forty years ago in Brooklyn. Of the others, Leo Ross was almost a New Yorker, having been born in Nassau County, Long Island, thirty-two years ago, while Cary Lane, twenty-eight, was from Los Angeles, and David Poumon, twenty-four, had originally been a resident of Toronto.

There were brief character analyses of all of them, and though I supposed they came from horoscopes rather than observation of the individuals, they seemed reasonably accurate in regard to the three I'd already met, describing Lane as "sociable, spontaneous, affectionate, imaginative, naïve, a follower, undisciplined, not interested in material things," David Poumon as "cerebral, nervous, flexible, abstract, carnal, intellectually curious, a loner, instinctive," and Stewart Remington as "emotional, visionary, facile, sensual, melancholy, passionate, combative, materialistic, dominating, driven." I didn't know whether all those words applied or not, but none of them seemed to me contradictory to my first impressions, so I read the descriptions of the other three with more interest than their source might otherwise have warranted:

Henry Koberberg: "balanced, intellectual, practical, constrained, susceptible, overly modest, passive, organizer, antidisciplinarian, emotionally harmonious."

Bruce Maundy: "passionate, aggressive, courageous, generous, ambitious, rebellious, voluptuous, inventive, hasty, headstrong, frank, financially prodigal, a gambler."

Leo Ross: "charming, diffuse, impulsive, clever, imaginative, expressive, generous, imprecise, superficial, social, sentimental, sexually dominating, financially unconcerned."

None of the six said "Murderous." Unfortunate.

There was more that Cornell had done, astrologically. Jamie Dearborn, born in April, was an Aries, and Cornell had decided—I couldn't quite figure out why—that somehow Aries was the key to the murder. He had put down all the suspects' connections with Aries, in phrases the meaning of which I was very vague about. Henry Koberberg had "Uranus in Aries," Cary Lane had "Aries ascendant," Bruce Maundy had "Mercury in Aries," David Poumon had both "Moon in Aries" and "Mars in Aries," Stewart Remington had both "Uranus in Aries" and "Venus in Aries," and Leo Ross had "Venus in Aries." (Dearborn, besides having been born under the sign of Aries, also had "Mercury in Aries" and "Aries ascendant," which may have had something to do with

Cornell's theory, I don't know.)

Well, we all had our methods for going forward once the logic and the facts ran out. Cornell's was to go poking in among the stars; mine was to go poking into the suspects' heads. Who can say which was the more irrational? I would see all six of these people tomorrow night, sometime after nine P.M., in the Brooklyn Heights apartment shared by Stewart Remington and Jerry Weissman.

It was now after four in the morning. Reluctantly, exhausted, I put the papers back in their envelope and went to bed. Kate moved in her sleep, but didn't awaken, when I crawled in beside her. The sheets, which had been cold on my side of the bed, gradually warmed. My mind, which had been spinning with thoughts on homosexuality, on astrology, on murder, on psychology, on detection, on belonging, on solitude, gradually slowed. I slept.

8

But I met another of my suspects sooner than I'd expected.

I got up late the next day, Saturday, and had breakfast as Kate and Bill were having lunch. Kate asked me about the evening before, naturally, partly because she was interested and partly because she always hopes to fire my own interest, and I told her a somewhat edited version of what I'd seen and the people I'd met, down-playing the homosexual aspects, the fact that these men were mostly living together in pairs, that one of them claimed to have been taking part in homosexual group sex at a public bath during the time of the attack on Cornell, that the homosexuality which gave their community whatever cohesiveness it might have (less, I suspected, than Jerry Weissman believed or wanted to believe) was also probably the central factor behind the motivation for Dearborn's murder. My story, though edited, did get through to her, as I could tell from some of her questions.

And in the process of answering those questions I was surprised to find my attention turning away from the subject at hand and focusing instead on Bill, sitting at the table to my left, listening to every word.

Bill, my only child—William Blair Tobin, that being Kate's maiden name in the middle—is fifteen now and still a healthy open boy of a style that seems hopelessly old-fashioned. He was on the high-school baseball team, a husky cheerful boy an inch taller than me, and I couldn't help looking at him from time to time and wondering what I might be—uncontrollably—doing to him. Our household atmosphere was much of the time silent and tense and empty, because of me. Although we had never talked about my having been thrown off the force, Bill and I, he did know the reason for it; for two or three days my multiple betrayals—of wife, of partner, of my uniform, of myself, in a way even of him—had been the joy of the tabloids.

And what did Bill think of it all? What did he think of the life we three lived in this house? What effect would it all some day have on him?

I don't know if I can be proved right or wrong, but I hold to the belief that homosexuality almost always shows a failure of some kind on the part of the parents. The failure of the father to be a man, or of the mother to be a woman, or of both to give their child security and love. Whatever the particular style of the failure, I think it almost always lies in the parents when the son emerges to adulthood as a homosexual.

Bill? Could that be what I'd done to him? Watching him now, with the memory fresh in my mind of the people I'd met last night, I was suddenly hypersensitive to every nuance of his expression, every slightest move of his hands or head. Was there anything there? His hair and clothing were in the normal style of teenagers these days—I am not one of those parents who insists on sending his child off to school dressed and shorn as though a time warp existed outside the front door and the child would find himself a classmate of the father—and the differences between today's youth styles and today's homosexual styles are frequently more narrow than a man of my generation can readily espy. But what of his manner? Were there any clues?

But that was foolishness, and in reality I knew it. There was not the slightest sign of homosexuality in Bill, there never had been, and I had no true reason to suppose there ever would be. I was simply adding fronds again to the landscape of my guilt.

After breakfast I went down to the basement again and to my new project. Bill had gone out somewhere and Kate was upstairs running the vacuum cleaner; I could hear it faintly, just at the threshold of hearing.

I did about an hour of work, finishing the concrete-block work I'd left off with yesterday, and then starting again to dig. I heard the doorbell clearly, heard the vacuum cleaner shut off, did not hear it start again. I paid no attention, and went on with my work. I would say I was successfully thinking about nothing.

The basement door opened. Kate called, "Mitch?"

I straightened, resting the shovel blade into the ground. I work very hard, and whenever I'm interrupted I discover I'm sweating and breathing heavily. But it keeps me from putting on weight; I suppose I should be happy for that. I called, "What is it?"

"There's someone here to see you. I told him you were busy, and he insisted. He said to tell you his name is Bruce Maundy, and he won't go away until he sees you."

Bruce Maundy. One of the six, the attempted playwright, currently working for a ticket agency in Manhattan. I remembered him from Cornell's papers, he was the only one who didn't live with another man, he lived in Queens—possibly around here somewhere—with his mother.

What had the astrological profile been? I could only remember a few of the words: "passionate, ambitious, headstrong, a gambler."

"I'll be up in five minutes," I said.

"All right." She shut the door again.

When working I keep my watch in my pants pocket so it

won't get scratched or knocked around. I took it out now, made a mental note of the time, put the watch back in my pocket, and returned to my digging. If Bruce Maundy was, as the stars proclaimed, passionate and ambitious and head-strong and a gambler—and for him to come beard me in my den suggested he was probably all of those things—it would do him good to wait five minutes; give him a chance to cool a bit.

The next time I checked my watch, seven minutes had passed. I put down the shovel, removed my work gloves, and went upstairs. In the kitchen I changed from sneakers to slippers and went over to the sink to wash up.

He hadn't cooled. He came lunging into the kitchen, a stocky strong-looking young man with a wild frizz of brown hair out from his head like an exaggerated parody of the style among blacks called Afro; except it wouldn't be a conscious parody and he himself might call what he was wearing an Afro. In which case I was wearing a Euro, I suppose.

On his feet were boots, vaguely cowboyish. He was wearing dungarees that looked to have been artificially faded; they had bell bottoms. He was also wearing a dungaree jacket open over a lime-green turtleneck sport shirt. Two sets of wood-and-stone beads hung around his neck, and on his face were eyeglasses with octagonal yellow lenses and plain wire frames.

He said, "I want to talk to you!" He sounded belligerent, and desperate.

I said, "I've been working. I am washing up. When I am finished washing up I will come see you in the living room."

"I can talk to you right here."

"But I can't listen," I said, and turned my back on him, and continued to wash my face and hands and arms. He talked; I didn't listen.

When he grabbed at my shoulder, I turned and slapped him backhand across the face. "I don't know what idea you have, Maundy," I said, "but you'll behave yourself in my house."

"Little tin father figure, is that it?"

"Before delivering the speech," I said, "that links me with Hitler, Duvalier and the Pentagon, let me point out that if you have something to say to me—"

"You're goddam right I have something to say!"

"—you've chosen," I finished, "the worst possible way to get me to listen."

"I don't like to be accused," he said, and jabbed himself in the chest with his thumb. "I don't like people prying into my life. I don't like it when the cops do it even *with* a warrant, and I sure as hell don't like it when some stumblebum like you does it."

"Does what?"

"Don't crap with me," he said. "I don't take hype, I really don't. That jerk Cornell gave you a list."

"He's a jerk?"

"Some investigation," he said with angry scorn. "He can't even get people's *horoscopes* right. And he gave you a list."

"Yes, he did."

"My name's on it."

"That's right."

"Well, get it the hell off it," he said. "You want to make lists, make a list of everybody driving on the Brooklyn Bridge that night. Maybe one of them saw it happen through the window. But don't make any list with *me* on it, or you're in for trouble."

I said, "Give me a reason to take your name off, and I'll be happy to."

"Because I'm *telling* you! You're the guy I read about in

my horoscope, that was gonna try to give me a bad time. Well, I don't *take* bad times, see? Those faggots can play their little games with each other all they want, but they can keep me the hell out of it. And that goes for you, too!"

I said, "You aren't a faggot?"

"I said you can keep me out of it! *Out* of it!"

"You don't want your mother to know, is that it?"

He was heading directly for uncontrollable rage. Before we left this kitchen, I was going to have to hit him very hard in order to keep him from hitting me. I knew it was going to happen, and he didn't, which was the only edge I had on him.

Now he said, "My mother? You think you can pressure me, you son of a bitch? You want to call her? Go ahead! Call her on the phone, tell her any smutty damn thing you can think of. What *I'm* talking about is individual liberty, and I do mean privacy, and I mean *you* stay out of my *life!*"

His dare was an obvious and pathetic bluff—the tremble in his body and voice was only partly rage, the rest was ill-disguised fear—but I didn't call him on it. Instead I stayed with the main point, saying, "But what if you killed Jamie Dearborn?"

He was speechless for a few seconds; just long enough to drop an octave, but not long enough to get some sense. "You're really asking for it," he said from between clenched teeth.

"I've never seen you before," I told him. "You come into my house, you claim to be Bruce Maundy, you talk inco—"

"*Claim* to be? What the hell are you, insane? What do you mean *claim* to be?"

"You talk incoherently," I said, "and make silly, impossible demands. You don't behave at all—"

"Wait a second, wait a second. Claim to be? I am Bruce—and what do you mean impossible demands? What kind of jerk are you? You want to see who I am?" And he started pawing in his hip pocket.

"You don't behave at all rationally," I said, "and if I'd been hired simply to find some patsy to take—"

"Here. Here. Here's who I am." Incredibly enough, he was waving his wallet in my face, showing me his driver's license.

"Some patsy," I repeated, "to take Cornell's place, my personal choice for the job would be you, and only partially because I've taken an instant dislike to you."

The wallet lowered, and he glared at me. "Oh, yeah? What are you talking about?"

"The fact of the matter is," I said, "you obviously came in here hoping to get my back up. You've succeeded, you're good at it."

"*Your* back up? People poking into my private life, you think—"

"So I suppose," I said, drowning him out with stronger projection, "that means you've had a lot of practice at it. Getting people mad at you. You probably have some sort of record for brawling. It wouldn't take much to show that you're the right *kind* of person to be Dearborn's killer. You don't have an alibi, and I'm sure I could count on you to wise-off to any police offi—"

I thought he'd turn out to be a headhunter, and I was right. I stepped inside the punch he aimed at my face and hit him twice just above the belt. He made the sound men make when the wind has just been punched out of them, and took two faltering steps backward before sitting down hard on the floor.

He didn't give up easily. Even before he could breathe again he was gesticulating, trying to say things. I waited until he'd managed the first deep breath, and then I went over and reached down and took his right thumb in my left hand.

There's a way to hold a person's thumb that is called the come-along hold. You have it bent down at the knuckle, and if you apply a little pressure, it hurts very much. You hold a person that way, say, "Come along," apply a little pressure, and they come along.

I said, "Come along."

We went into the living room, where I sat him in an arm-chair and stood in front of him to say, "We've used your system so far; shouts and fighting. Now we'll use mine."

"Boy, I can believe you used to be a cop," he said. His voice was hoarse, his manner lowering and still belligerent. "You never get over the taste for it, do you?"

"If we're going to go on using your system," I said, "maybe we'd better go downstairs, where we won't bother my wife. Do you want to come along, or do you want to try things my way?"

He was nursing his thumb. "What choice do I have?"

"To be a fool or a grownup," I said. "You're twenty-six years old, isn't it time you stopped pretending you were about to liberate a campus?"

He didn't say anything to that, just glared at me. He was going to be sullen now.

I was tired of him. I said, "You have no alibi for the time when Dearborn was killed. But if you have one for the time Cornell was attacked, I'll be happy to take you off my list."

I waited. He said nothing. He had put the thumb in his mouth.

I said, "Maundy, this isn't a bus depot. If you have nothing to say to me, get up and leave."

"I've said what I'm going to say."

"Then leave."

He hesitated, reluctant to take any of the options open to

him. Finally, squinting up at me as though we were in bright sunlight, he said, "It's nobody's business where I was Monday."

"Not if you weren't at Jammer."

"I don't want you poking around, or you're likely to get yourself in big trouble."

"You'd better get out of here now," I said. "You're beginning to repeat yourself."

"You really think you're tough."

"If you really want me to throw you out physically," I said, "I will."

"I'm going," he said, blustering. "Don't worry, I don't want to hang around here any more than I have to." He got to his feet, shrugging his shoulders around in his denim jacket as though to impress himself with his cowboy toughness. "Just you forget about me and Monday," he said. "That's all you got to know."

I walked him to the front door, where he had a Navy pea jacket and an African safari hat. He put them on, pulled on racing-driver gloves, glared at me while trying to think of an exit line, failed to find one, and left. I saw him stomp out toward an old rusted white MG with a racing rollbar, and I shut the door.

As I started down the hall, I heard the vacuum cleaner begin again upstairs. I smiled upward; Kate had been listening. I went on to the kitchen, and back down to my work.

9

It had started to snow again after dinner, another slow and lazy fall, without wind. It hadn't amounted to much yet, but if it kept on like this, it would count as a real storm by morning.

Driving, at ten in the evening, was still no problem, but finding a parking space in Brooklyn Heights, as always, was. I walked nearly four blocks from the car to the address shared by Stewart Remington and Jerry Weissman. I had my hat pulled down and my coat collar turned up, but the slow-descending snowflakes still managed from time to time to get through to the back of my neck. And when I turned in at Remington's building my hat and shoulders were covered completely with a dusting of white.

The building was similar to Cornell's, except that at some point in its seventy or eighty years of life the high stone outside steps had been removed, and the main entrance had been switched to the ground floor. From the design of the tile-and-glass entryway, I would guess the alteration had been made shortly after the Second World War.

I could hear the party from the sidewalk. I had purposely chosen to come late, after the party was already in full swing, so that my entrance could be more unobtrusive and I would have a better chance to observe without being observed.

The party was in full swing, all right. I had to ring twice before someone came to let me in. Looking through the glass at a cream-colored corridor, I saw a youngish Negro with a restrained Afro haircut and a bushy mustache come out of the door at the far end and wave to me that he was coming. He was dressed, I noticed, almost conservatively, in suit and tie and ordinary oxford shoes. Of course, the suit lapels were shaped a bit oddly and the tie was very wide and many different colors, and his shirt was canary-yellow, but at least he was in a suit, and so was I; I wouldn't be entirely out of place.

(It had been difficult deciding what to wear tonight. Would I be more unobtrusive in my regular clothing, no matter how anachronistic I might look against the other guests, or should I dress myself, at least partly, out of Bill's closet? I finally decided I would feel best appearing as myself, so that's what I'd done.)

The Negro came and opened the door, laughing at the snow on me. "Now that's what I call a white man," he said.

I took my hat off and looked at it. "You mean a wet man," I said.

He shut the door and looked keenly at me. "I probably mean Tobin, don't I? Mitch Tobin?"

"That's right."

He grinned. "You see? I penetrated your disguise."

"Very clever of you. I'm afraid you have the advantage of me; I haven't penetrated yours yet."

"Nobody has," he said. Was there a touch of self-mockery in his smile for a second? He extended a hand toward me, saying, "I'm Leo Ross." And then, in a dramatic hoarse whisper, grinning all the while, "Suspect."

"Oh, yes," I said, and took his hand. "I've been looking forward to meeting you."

"And isn't that the truth," he said. "Do you want to grill me now, or wait and boil me later?"

"If you have an alibi for nine o'clock Monday evening," I

said, "I'd love to hear it right now and cross your name off the list."

"Monday evening." The smile never entirely left his face, but seemed to hang there for a moment without his volition while he thought of other things. "An alibi," he said, "means that other people saw me where I say I was."

"That's right."

"Then I don't have one." A helpless smile, a spreading of the hands. "I wish I could help you out."

Why could none of these people take this thing seriously? One of their number was dead. Another was in the hospital, and well on his way to being railroaded into an asylum.

I remembered a few of the words in the astrological description of Leo Ross: "charming, clever, superficial, sexually dominating." I didn't know about the last, but the others seemed to apply. I said, "Where were you, that you can't prove?"

"In church." The smile grew wistful for a second, as though he had trouble himself believing he'd been in church, but then it disappeared entirely, and very earnestly he said, "I've been doing a novena to the Sacred Heart. For world peace. Nine days, eight-thirty each evening. It was over Thursday."

"And you went alone?"

"Henry isn't Catholic." Then he laughed and said, "We don't know *how* we'll bring up the children."

"You don't know anyone else in the congregation."

"Not a soul. And it's a big old church, stone, very dark, and not many people come to novenas any more. We tend to scatter around the place. Someone *might* remember seeing me there, but I doubt it. And if they did, how could they be sure which night it was? No, I'm sorry, I'm going to be a problem for you."

"We'll work it out," I assured him. "Somehow."

"I do believe you will," he said, peering at me. "You don't go ha ha as much as most people."

It was a strange description; it drew a chuckle from me, which may have been its intention. In any case, Ross promptly grew frothy and cheerful again, saying, "But the party isn't out here, it's inside. Come join the festivities." He took my arm, and we went in together.

10

It was impossible to get much of an idea of the apartment; it was too full of people, most of them giving the appearance of having bought their clothes at Jammer. I was more than an anachronism here, in my dark gray suit and slender figured tie, I was a fantasy from an entirely different world.

It was strange, but that was the effect the party had on me. Not that *they* were fantasies, though some of them were in out-and-out drag, feminine pants suits and coifed hair and false eyelashes and make-up and earrings, but that *I* was the fantasy, intruding on their reality. Because they were the majority, I suppose, and I was alone.

Ross shouted in my ear, "Drinks through that doorway! Want to talk to Henry?"

Henry Koberberg, he meant, his partner and the sixth suspect on the list. I nodded, he nodded back with a big smile, and he was off and I was alone.

But not for long. Stewart Remington emerged from the surge of guests like a luxury liner out of a fog bank. He extended his hand to be shaken—I noticed again the lack of strength in it—and leaned close to bellow, in an even deeper baritone than usual, "Jerry told me he invited you!"

I shouted back, "I hope it's all right with you."

"It's fine with me!" he yelled. "Manzoni's going into court on Monday! Anything you do is fine with me!"

I nodded, rather than shout again.

He waved an arm—I noticed that tonight he was wearing a cape, waist-length, blue, white satin lining—and roared, "Drinks through that door over there!"

I nodded my thanks, he gave me a meaningless nod and wink and smile, and off he went into the fog bank again, patting shoulders and cheeks as he went.

I saw no one I recognized. The room was long, but rather narrow, and there were probably twenty-five people present, all standing, all drinking, but less than half smoking. They were in five or six fluctuating conversational groups, and it was obvious that all these people knew one another, that I was the only one meeting the group for the first time.

They all seemed so *happy*. Watching them, I thought at first it was a kind of hysterical happiness, urgent and artificial: Germany in the twenties. But it wasn't that, or at least I soon stopped thinking so. What I finally decided was that the apparent artificiality and overstatement came from the fact that these people were more expressive and outwardly emotional than most men. To be in a room full of men dressed like South American birds and chattering like a beauty salon made for a certain sense of dislocation; it became difficult to say what was a normal level of behavior and what was strain.

Leo Ross had not returned with Henry Koberberg. Stewart Remington was no longer in sight. I caught a quick glimpse of Cary Lane, blond hair gleaming as he pirouetted in the middle of a conversational group at the far end of the room, but then people moved in the intervening space and I lost him again. David Poumon and Bruce Maundy were supposed to be here as well, but I didn't see either of them.

There was steady traffic in both directions through the doorway that both Ross and Remington had pointed out to me, so after a minute or two I headed in that direction, skirting along the edge of the room and getting only a couple of questioning glances from people I passed. Most of the partygoers were deeply involved in their conversations or in one another or simply in their own reactions to things.

I got to the doorway finally, started through, and bumped into Bruce Maundy, who was coming out, carrying two high-ball glasses with iced drinks. He was in a blue turtleneck sweater tonight, black trousers, and a wide glittering silvery belt that looked like an outsized wristwatch expansion band.

His reaction was immediate; he glared at me, glared at the drinks in his hands as though they were the only things keeping him from throwing himself at my throat, glared at me again, and leaned close to my face to snarl at me through clenched teeth, saying, "I told you to stay away from me."

"I was invited here," I said. I preferred not to have a scene in public; it would complicate the work I had to do.

"You won't follow me around any more," he said, and brushed by me with more than the necessary roughness.

I watched him, hoping to see who the other drink was for, but I lost sight of him midway through the room. Also, I was blocking the doorway for other drinkers, so I continued on through into a fairly small room with yellow-and-white wallpaper, antique-looking white sideboard and hutch, and a long table against one wall covered with glasses and bottles and a couple of ice buckets. Half a dozen guests were grouped at the table, and it seemed as though every time one left with a replenished drink, another one would take his place. But none of them the people I was interested in.

I moved on, and in the kitchen I found Jerry Weissman washing glasses. Up to his elbows in dishwater. He grinned at me and called, "Hi! You just get here?"

"A few minutes ago." The noise level was way down in the kitchen, making it possible to speak in normal tones.

Jerry Weissman held his soapy hands up for me to see,

saying with humorous resignation, "Isn't it always the way? People drink a drink halfway, put their glass down, forget where they put it, and go make another drink in another glass. So you've got to keep on washing glasses all the time. You could wind up with dishpan hands."

Since he had undoubtedly volunteered for the job, and since in all likelihood it was unnecessary—there had seemed to be plenty of clean glasses still on the table in the other room—I didn't waste time sympathizing with him, but said, "I don't seem to be finding the people I want."

"Really?" He frowned, puzzled. "I think they're all here."

"I saw Remington, and Bruce Maundy. And I caught a glimpse of Cary Lane."

"The others are here. David is always nearby to Cary. And Leo and Henry have to be around someplace."

"Leo was the one who let me in. Actually, Henry Koberberg is the only one I'm not sure of. I don't know what he looks like."

"Do you want me to come point him out?"

"If you would, I'd appreciate it."

"Sure." He shook suds from his hands and reached for a towel, then stopped and said, "Hey, I know where he is. Upstairs."

"Upstairs?"

"Up in the library. He doesn't really like parties, he comes because of Leo. But then he heads for whatever room has books."

"And that would be upstairs?"

"You know the door you came in? Not the outer door, the one to the living room."

"Yes."

"Right next to it there's another door. That leads to the

stairs. The library's to the back."

"Second floor?"

"Yeah, we've only got the two. Stew rents out the top two."

"Thank you." I started for the door.

"He has a beard," Weissman said.

"Thanks."

11

I interrupted a couple necking on the stairs. They weren't embarrassed, and in fact both made jokes about it while I stepped over them, suddenly all knees. And one of them was so completely in female drag that I was past them before it occurred to me that both were men.

I thought, *I should feel disgusted*, but I didn't, I felt nothing about it at all. I had as much reaction as I would have to seeing an automobile go by in the street. But then, as I neared the top of the stairs, I finally did have a reaction of sorts: surprise. At myself. I had always thought that in eighteen years on the New York police force, I had seen just about everything there was to see, but I had never before in my life seen two homosexuals kiss. And now that I had, the only reaction I could dredge up was surprise at never having seen it happen before.

At the head of the stairs I was distracted by the sounds of voices. They weren't screaming, but they were harsh; two men were in an argument together, and there was just something about the voices that sounded as though it was a long-term argument, one that had started long ago and would not be settled now, not here, not tonight.

They were in the direction I'd been told to go. I went through a doorway, across a rather ordinary bedroom—particularly considering the rooms I'd been seeing the last few days—dominated by a king-size bed with a white spread and

105

several heart-shaped red pillows on it, and opened a door on the other side.

It was the library. The man standing was Leo Ross, and the man seated in the maroon leather chair, bearded, stout, pedantic-looking, would surely be Henry Koberberg.

I hadn't been able to make out any of the words through the closed door, but as I came through the doorway Ross was saying, "—never want to face up to—" at which point he became aware of me, grew very flustered, and stopped his pacing, his speech and his gestures all in mid-flow.

I said, "Excuse me. Jerry Weissman said I might find Mr. Koberberg in the library."

Koberberg looked at me with obvious dislike that he was obviously trying to hide. "I am Henry Koberberg," he said. He had a surprisingly light frail voice for his size and appearance.

Leo Ross had the nervousness of someone who wants to maintain the social appearances and is afraid the situation has gone beyond his control. "Henry," he said now, with false cheeriness, "this is Mitch Tobin."

"I know who he is," Koberberg said. He wasn't interested in social appearances, not really, which was why he couldn't hide his dislike for me.

"If you'd prefer to talk with me another time," I said, leaving the sentence up in the air, letting it tell him I intended us to have a conversation sooner or later, and waited for his response.

He considered me without pleasure, and finally nodded. "We might as well talk now. You won't need Leo, I suppose."

It didn't matter to me one way or the other, since I'd already talked with Ross when I first came in. If Koberberg preferred to converse with me without his partner being present, I didn't mind at all.

But Leo did. He took his dismissal poorly, giving Koberberg an angry look before saying to me, silkily, "I'll probably see you downstairs later."

"Fine," I said.

Ross left, and a little silence settled down between Koberberg and me, mostly because Koberberg didn't meet my eye, but sat gazing thoughtfully at the door Ross had just shut behind him. Finally he said, "This is a bad time to be a black man, of course. The first generation with dignity has the most trouble." He offered me a wintry smile, saying, "Don't you think so?"

"I have no idea what you're talking about," I said.

"Until very recently," he explained pedantically, "it was impossible for a black man to fail, because nobody expected him to succeed at anything. While the rest of us had the three choices of success or the status quo or failure, the black man only had the choices of success or status quo. Now, very suddenly, that has changed. The black man is *expected* to join the struggle for success today; success is no longer a bolt from heaven. Since he is expected to struggle, it now becomes possible for him to fail. The first generation to greet the possibility of failure, which means the possibility of success, which means dignity, has the most difficulty of adjustment."

I wasn't sure his reasoning was entirely seamless, but I saw no point in getting lost in a discussion that wasn't what I was here for, so I angled the topic back by saying, "Is that why Ross was angry just now?"

"It's at the seat, I believe," he said, "of most of his displays of temper. He is a very petulant boy, really. I would dismiss most of what he says, were I you."

I said, "And Jamie Dearborn? Did he suffer from the same thing?"

Koberberg's smile hinted at reminiscence, but what he

said was, "Not at all. Jamie was a success, and he knew it. The question had been answered, which is to say the transition was complete."

I said, "Who hated him?"

Koberg beamed, a big happy face. "Almost everybody," he said.

"Including you?"

"He frequency irritated me. His manner was abrasive. The first generation has the most trouble assimilating success, as well. He was a poor winner."

"What did he do to you?"

Koberg stopped smiling, and looked down at his rather large stomach. "Do? He didn't *do* anything. Nothing you could measure, or describe, or copy down in shorthand. He simply contrasted us for his pleasure and my embarrassment." He raised eyes that looked as though they would have shown pain if they had shown anything. But they didn't show anything.

The door behind me opened. I turned my head, and Cary Lane came in, his expression guileless and happy. *His* expression? How could you tell what his expression was, ever? How could you tell anything about Cary Lane, ever, by looking at the face he'd bought?

Lane said, "Am I interrupting?" He said it as though he knew he was, didn't much care, and didn't believe anyone would take an interruption from *him* seriously anyway.

Koberg said, "Come in, Cary. We were talking about what a pleasant disposition Jamie had."

"Oh, you." Lane went—"flounced" isn't quite the word— over to the bookshelves and pretended to read the spines.

"Now, as to Cary," Koberg said, "he *does* have a pleasant disposition. Don't you, Cary?"

"I'm sweet clear through," Lane told him, and turned his

108

head to wink at me.

"No, he really is," Koberberg insisted. "Because he has everything he wants. Don't you, Cary?"

"I have my David," Lane said, this time keeping his back to us and pretending deep absorption in book spines.

"Yes, you have," Koberberg said pleasantly. "And you have your career. And you have your good looks."

I found myself wondering if Lane's face would age like an ordinary face, or if it would remain smooth and plastic and unlined forever, while the body around it gradually aged and finally died and eventually rotted. And a graverobber a thousand years from now would find bones and dust and a perfect seamless sunny smiling face.

I said to Koberberg, "Ross tells me he went to a novena Monday night."

Koberberg nodded, pursing his lips. "He tells me the same."

"You don't believe him?"

"Sometimes I do, sometimes I don't."

Lane faced us again, saying, "Oh, I *am* interrupting."

"Not at all," I said to him. "Did Jamie Dearborn ever do anything unkind to you?"

"To me?" The perfect face expressed astonishment. "Good heavens, what for?"

"Weren't you competitors?"

"No no no! Because we're both models? But our styles are entirely different! They would *never* have sent Jamie out on an assignment that would be right for me."

"And vice versa?"

The perfect face went blank. "I beg your pardon?" He reminded me then of Carol Channing.

"Would they send you out on an assignment," I explained, "that would be right for Jamie?"

109

"How could they? Do I look like a token black man?"

Koberberg barked with laughter, clapping his hands together. "Well spoken, Cary! Very good!"

I said to Lane, "Did Jamie ever go to the ballet with you?"

"Oh, no. I told you, I prefer to go alone."

"Would you say you and Jamie were friends?"

"Oh, yes!" The face was still guileless, for whatever that was worth.

Koberberg said, dryly, "You may leave us now, Cary. If we say anything about David, I will let you know."

Lane looked flustered. "I was just looking for a book," he said.

Koberberg shook his head. "Cary, what on earth would you do with a book?"

Now Lane did show that he was stung. "Oh, you," he said, "you think you're the only one in the world with brains."

"Not the only one," Koberberg said. "But one of the very few." He gave Lane his wintry smile, and waited.

Lane couldn't figure out an exit. He made uncompleted gestures toward the bookshelves, then shrugged awkwardly and said, "Well, I'll come back later, then. Sorry if I interrupted." The last said with heavy sarcastic overtones.

"Maybe we can talk later," I said to him as he went by me.

He gave me a surprised smile. "I'd like that," he said, sounding as though he really would, and left.

Koberberg, looking at the door, said, "And that's why Cary's still alive and Jamie's dead."

"Personality?"

"Of course."

"What was Jamie's personality?"

"I understand he was an Aries, but I would say he had the personality of a scorpion. Not Scorpio, scorpion."

"Are you involved in astrology, too?"

"We all are, to an extent. The complexities of the modern world, you know. The search for the authoritarian father figure becomes steadily more baroque. Our Father, Who art in Heaven. Yes? In the heavens, then, in the stars. And He will tell us what to do; all we have to do is listen closely to the music of the celestial spheres."

"You don't take it seriously?"

"Sometimes I do, sometimes I don't."

"Like Ross's novena," I said.

He gave a snort of surprised laughter. "Are we back there again? Oh, I suppose Leo was at his grubby novena, he does do that sort of thing. In any event, he wasn't killing anybody. Not Jamie, not Ronnie."

"Why not?"

"Leo suffers at the hands of others," he said. "It would take away some of his pleasure to cut down on the number of hands."

"In other words, you say he's a masochist."

"I find labels embarrassing," he said. "Leo doesn't like to be whipped, which is the implication I get from that particular label. But his life-style is to be mistreated by other people and to miss opportunities for success because of the distraction and agony of that mistreatment. It's Leo's individual answer to the problem of having success thrust upon him as an alternative."

"Are you one of the people who mistreat him?"

A smile with down-turned corners, a shake of the head: "I am Leo's father figure. I am the one whose task it is to tell him he should succeed anyway, no matter what the bad people do."

"What were you arguing about, before I came in?"

"He wanted me to see you. I didn't want to see you."

"Why not?"

"I find your line of work distasteful. As bad as psychoanalysis, in its way. I am a very private person, Mr. Tobin, I think of myself as a desk with many small drawers, each containing some small private treasure of value and interest to no one but me. I don't want you poking about in my drawers, if you'll forgive an inadvertent sexual remark. Under other circumstances, perhaps we would get along, would have inspiriting conversations together. But when you come to me with one purpose in mind, to peel me open and pluck tiny facts out of me, you make me extremely uncomfortable. I would have preferred to avoid this meeting altogether. Failing which, I notice that my tactic has been to smother you in words."

"I don't mind," I said. "Ross argued against you?"

"As you heard. He was afraid you would think me guilty if I refused to talk with you. But I'm on your suspect list anyway, am I not?"

I said, "Who do you think killed Dearborn?"

"I have no idea."

"Do you agree with Cornell's list?"

"I don't know that I know the list entirely. Leo and I are on it, Cary is on it, David Poumon is on it."

"Stewart Remington and Bruce Maundy."

His face brightened. "Those two! Both of them? I have nothing to fear!" He looked and sounded as though he were only half-joking.

I said, "You think it's one of them?"

"Either or both," he said. "Both violent, both bad-tempered, both strong and active. Arrest them both and try them alternately."

"I'm not a policeman."

"Yes, I know. And I am not really homosexual." He smiled at me.

"I mean I'm not on the force."

"I know what you mean."

112

"Do you have an alibi for Monday?"

"Of course not. Would Leo have been so upset?"

"What do you think he was doing Monday?"

"He? Leo?"

"Yes."

"He was at the novena, as he said."

"And if he wasn't?"

A shadow crossed his face. He contemplated not answering me at all, I could see that, and when he spoke he said, "That's the sort of thing I meant before. You want to pull all the little facts into the open air."

"Do you think he has a lover somewhere, is that it?"

He laughed aloud, harshly. "*A* lover! Do you know what the word 'cruise' means?"

"In this context," I said, gesturing to include the building we were in, "it would mean walking around some specific section of the city trying to pick somebody up. Somebody homosexual."

"Yes," he said. "Very good."

"Ross cruises?"

"I have never said so. I have never entirely articulated the thought. Do you wish to force me to?"

I said, "Where were *you* Monday night?"

"We have a shop on the first floor," he said. "In back, we restore old furniture. I was there, working on a Bentwood chair. Alone, naturally."

I said, "Did Jamie cruise?"

"God knows."

"You must know," I said. "You people know almost everything about one another."

"Ronnie believes that Jamie was faithful," he said carefully. "I have never seen anything to lead me to believe he's wrong."

"Why do you say it like that? Why keep a little bit back?"

"Probably," he said, "because I can't really believe the little bastard was true to anybody. Possibly, after Leo, I can't believe that any black man can be faithful. Probably because I would prefer to think badly of Jamie in every possible way. You see how you have me opening drawers? I hope, once this conversation is over, it will never be necessary for you and me to meet again."

"Would you like to end it now?"

"I would like it to have never begun. But now that it is, let's make it as encyclopedic as possible, and get it over with forever."

I said, "Why does Cary Lane think David Poumon killed Dearborn?"

He looked surprised. "You noticed that? I wonder what you've noticed about me."

"Do you know why?"

"I have no idea. I would tell you if I did."

"Who do you think did it?"

"The only one I can think of," he said, "who disliked Jamie strongly enough to want to see him dead was me. And I didn't do it, so I'm at a loss."

"Thank you," I said. Turning away, I put my hand on the doorknob, then looked back at him and said, "You really don't have to be that cautious. You're better than you think you are."

His smile was bitter. "Next, you'll be telling me I'm strong enough to go to the party. My Fuehrer, I can walk!"

If he preferred himself as he was, I'd be wasting my time saying anything more. Besides, that wasn't what I was here for. "Thank you for your time," I said, and left him.

12

David Poumon was at the bar in the small yellow room downstairs. I went over and stood beside him and made myself a
drink. I discovered a long time ago that dry vermouth on ice
makes an acceptable drink that can be sipped over a long period of time without having much of any effect, so that's what
I made for myself now.

Poumon noticed me, said hello, and I said hello back. I
thought he was going to let the conversation lapse right there,
but when he picked up his drink—something and ginger ale
—he said, "Are you learning things?"

"I'm still in the first stage," I said. "I'm learning what
questions to ask."

That was an obvious lead-in; the long hesitation he made
before making the inevitable response told me he believed he
had things to hide. But so have we all, to one extent or
another. Did his concern murder, or was he simply another
one like Henry Koberberg, afraid primarily of being forced to
be self-aware?

In any event, he finally did make the response I'd been
angling for: "What kind of questions?"

"For instance," I said casually, "why your friend Cary
thinks you're the one who killed Dearborn."

He frowned at me, but didn't show much surprise. Some
people came over, wanting to make drinks, and we separated
slightly as we moved to the opposite corner of the room, near

the kitchen doorway but out of the general flow of traffic. Then he said, "If that's supposed to be a clever trick, I think it's kind of dumb."

"No trick," I said. "It's a question that's come up, that's all, and I'd like to find an answer to it if I could."

"The thing that's wrong with that," he said, "is that Cary wouldn't ever say such a silly thing. Not even if he thought it."

"I didn't say he said it. I said he thought it."

"You read minds?" He wasn't angry with me so much as he was contemptuous and disappointed; he'd thought more of me than this.

I said, "Have you ever found it really very hard to read Cary Lane's mind?"

"I've known Cary a long time."

"Look," I said, "I have no more reason to think you're a murderer than I did when we met last night. You say you were at home working on your music when Cornell was attacked, and I have no reason so far to believe otherwise. I'm not saying that I believe Lane, I'm merely saying that Lane is afraid you killed Dearborn, and he's afraid I'll find out about it."

"I didn't kill him," Poumon said. "I've never killed anybody."

"I'll accept that, for the moment. But why does Lane think you did?"

"I don't know. Maybe he's afraid I'll be arrested and he'll lose me. How can I say what's inside his head?"

"Did you and Dearborn ever have a fight? An argument? Any kind of disagreement?"

He shook his head at all three.

I said, "What about Lane? They were both models, did *he* have trouble with Dearborn? Is he afraid you did it to revenge him, or something like that?"

He went on shaking his head, and when I was done, he said, "Neither Cary nor I had any reason to kill Jamie Dearborn."

"And yet he's afraid you did it."

"I'm sorry if he is, I don't like to see him upset. Particularly when there's no reason for it. Will you excuse me now?"

"Yes, of course," I said.

13

There were other conversations. I talked briefly with Stewart Remington, and he told me that I was the only one present who was not in some sort of financial arrangement with him, mostly through his law office. These were his clients, and he was prouder of them as clients than as friends. He pointed out those whose income tax he handled, those whose contracts and mortgages and wills he had taken care of, those who had him on an annual retainer.

I asked him about Jammer, and it emerged that he handled all the legal and financial arrangements for the store, from the lease for the building through the payment of local and state and federal taxes to the keeping of the books. Cornell kept the non-financial records for the store, but Remington served as the place's accountant. He had also sold them their fire and theft insurance.

And what about Jammer's financial health? Cornell had told him about the arrangement where I was to have a fifteen percent interest in the store if I produced the murderer, so Remington misunderstood my question to be mercenary in intent. He assured me that Jammer was doing fine, that my fifteen percent could only increase in value, and that the store had never had a financial worry of any kind. They had managed to get favorable mentions in two of the right men's magazines shortly after they'd opened, four years ago, and had never lost momentum.

When I asked him if either Dearborn or Cornell was extravagant, he laughed and waved an arm to include all his guests, saying, "Extravagance tends to be a way of life when you expect to have no heirs. We all love our plumage, even me."

"Could Dearborn have been in some sort of financial jam?"

"Definitely not. Between Jammer and his modeling fees, Jamie was making a minimum of forty thousand a year. Plus the real estate he and Ronnie own."

"Real estate?"

"Three houses here in the Heights."

"They'll be worth a lot of money."

"Close to four hundred thousand. Of course, most of that is tied up in mortgages. But the rentals cover expenses and leave a little profit."

"Cornell inherits?"

"In a way. It's not precisely like a marriage, of course. We drew up legal partnership papers on everything they did together. Jamie had a savings account in his own name; I believe that money will go back to his family in Omaha."

"How much?"

"About twelve thousand."

"Parents? Back in Omaha?"

"Two sisters, I believe."

"Do you know if he was in any kind of contact with them?"

"Ronnie could tell you for sure. I tend to doubt it. Jamie wasn't interested in the life he'd had before he came to New York."

I next began to ask him about my other suspects, but he refused to make any comments at all. "Whoever you wind up putting the finger on," he said, "will undoubtedly hire me to represent him. I feel I shouldn't discuss my future client with you."

"What if it turns out to be you?"

He looked surprised, then laughed his booming laugh and said, "Who *will* I get for my attorney? Excuse me, please." And he went off to laugh and talk and clap the backs of his clients. His guests.

I walked around, watching and listening, carrying my glass of vermouth. Twice, guests engaged me in conversation, both times patently trying to ease a certain curiosity about me. One of them said, "I never saw anybody in Warner Brothers drag before. It's fascinating." I didn't volunteer any facts about myself, nor did I cut the conversations short. I was as interested in their milieu as they were in mine. I would also have liked a casual word dropped about one or more of my suspects, but that didn't happen.

I saw most of my suspects as I walked around. Not Koberberg, of course, he would still be upstairs in the library, the remote-control chaperon of Leo Ross. But I did see Ross, a charming smile under his bushy mustache, in apparently seductive conversation with a slender young man with gray eye make-up and incredibly hollow cheeks. David Poumon and I crossed paths a few times, both of us nodding, neither speaking. Cary Lane fluttered by once or twice, always pausing to say something sprightly and cheerful. I considered asking him why he was so afraid about Poumon, but decided I would get no coherent answer, and let it go.

I didn't see Maundy anywhere. At first I wasn't actually looking for him, but eventually he became noticeable because of his absence, and then I did do an actual search, culminating in the kitchen, where Jerry Weissman was now in the process of preparing coffee in two large electric coffeemakers. Two cardboard boxes from a bakery stood on the table in the middle of the room, waiting to be opened.

I said, "Have you seen Bruce Maundy? Did he go upstairs?"

"Bruce?" He was like a very dedicated young student nurse, ready at all times to rush off on an errand. "He hasn't been through here. Sometimes he gets turned off and goes home early."

"Thanks."

"Coffee and cookies pretty soon," he announced, and I nodded and waved from the doorway, and went on back to the party.

A while later I saw Leo Ross emerging from the room with the bar in it. He was alone, and I intercepted him before he could return to his friend with the sunken cheeks. "Hello," I said, stepping in front of him, and he looked irritable for one brief second before tacking a carefree smile on his face. He said, "How did you and Henry get along?"

"Fine. He tells me you cruise when you're supposed to be at novenas."

The smile flicked out, and the irritability showed itself undisguised. "He did? What did he do that for?"

"Because it makes him sad, I suppose. The point is, for my purposes it would be better if you *were* cruising. If you were successful, I mean. That way, you'd have an alibi."

The smile returned, but this time intermixed with the irritation. "Sorry, my friend," he said. "Monday I was truly a good boy. I was really at the novena."

"It wouldn't have to be a public alibi," I said. "Koberberg wouldn't have to know about it. That's the advantage in my not really being a policeman."

"Another advantage," he said, his smile getting tighter all the time, "is that I don't have to talk to you." He stepped around me, and moved on.

14

I left the party a little after one. Except for Bruce Maundy, none of my suspects had yet departed; in fact, I was almost the first to leave. Jerry Weissman had attempted to distribute his coffee and cookies about an hour before, with very limited success, and the party I left was almost exactly the same as the party I'd arrived at three hours before. The same volume level, the same arrangements of standing conversational groups, the same chipper superficial chatter. I had expected, as the drinks were consumed, that some sort of change would take place, toward more happiness or toward some kind of trouble, but it hadn't happened and it looked now as though it wouldn't. If these people were most of them wearing masks, the masks seemed to be very securely in place; drink alone wouldn't dislodge them.

It was still snowing, as lazily and steadily as before. Walking the four blocks to where I'd parked my car, I tried to visualize Jamie Dearborn at that party. How would he have behaved? How would he have talked with the differing groups, with each of my differing suspects? That he would have disappeared in there like a minnow in a school of minnows I had no doubts, but what specific kind of minnow would he have been?

Jamie Dearborn had been clubbed to death, in a time-honored tradition, by a brass candlestick, a part of the décor of the top-floor bedroom in which the body had been found. I

tried to visualize each of my suspects wielding that candlestick, and at first I could see none of them doing it. But then,
as I thought about them further, I could see every one of them
swinging that shaped piece of brass at Jamie Dearborn's
head.

Stewart Remington judiciously.

Bruce Maundy enragedly.

Cary Lane hysterically.

David Poumon coldly.

Henry Koberberg agonizedly.

Leo Ross irritably.

There is no type of human being which is a killer type; all
men can kill, given the proper impetus.

If only I had met Jamie Dearborn in life, I would know
better what kind of impetus he would be likely to give, which
of the six he would be most likely to rub the wrong way.

The only one of them who had said anything against Dearborn was Koberberg, who had claimed Dearborn was generally disliked for being unpleasant in some way about his suc-
cesses in life. Did that make Koberberg my prime suspect?
Or, since he had talked about his feelings so plainly, did it
make him my least likely suspect?

I had to know more, and I wasn't even sure where to do my
looking.

Tomorrow I would visit Cornell again.

I suddenly wondered who would get Jammer and the three
houses if Cornell, too, were to die. I would have to remember
to ask him about that tomorrow.

And where would I find out Stewart Remington's current
financial condition? I didn't know, but it was probably worth
looking into.

I reached the car, my head full of notes and questions. I
cleared accumulated snow from the windshield, unlocked the

door, and slid in behind the wheel. I keep a notebook and pencil in the glove compartment, and now I wrote down in this all the questions I could think of that I wanted to try to find answers to tomorrow.

My best route home was over to the Brooklyn-Queens Expressway and out the Long Island Expressway. There was quite a bit of traffic out on the highways, as usual for a Saturday night, but it was fast-moving and made for easy driving. The roadway itself was clear of snow, for the most part.

It was as I took the exit ramp off the Long Island Expressway that I saw the flashing red light behind me. I knew I hadn't been exceeding the speed limit, and so I was certain the light wasn't for me. A few cars had passed me at fairly high speed; it would be one of them the patrol car was after.

Except that it followed me down the ramp. And it wasn't precisely a patrol car. It was a detective's car, which is to say it was an ordinary-appearing car with no police colorings or markings on it, and the red signal light was mounted on the dashboard just inside the windshield rather than on the roof.

And it was me he wanted. As I left the ramp and rolled out onto the street, this one fairly dark and completely deserted except for the two of us, he pulled up beside me and I saw him waving at me to pull over and stop. He was alone in the front seat, but there was another person in the back.

I stopped the car, and he angled to a stop in front of me. I didn't bother reaching for my wallet to get out my license, because I already believed this was something other than a normal traffic problem.

He was a burly man, made burlier by the heavy overcoat he wore. The falling snow made him somewhat indistinct as he walked heavily back toward me, but my impression was of a large, heavy-set man of about forty, in black overcoat and black hat.

I rolled my window down as he reached me. "Yes, Officer?"

His face was heavy, too, with the shadowed jaw of a man whose beard is too heavy for any razor. "License and registration," he said, mumbling the words from long practice.

Was it a normal traffic check after all? But it just didn't have the right feel to it, and in any case, uniformed patrolmen handle that sort of thing. I had the feeling I was meeting Detective Aldo Manzoni.

But I followed his lead, merely getting my license out of my wallet and my registration out of the glove compartment, and handing them to him. He stood in the snow, studying them, for an interminable time, and then stepped back a pace and said, "Would you get out of the car, please?"

I opened the door and stepped out.

"Shut the door, please." He had put my license and registration in his overcoat pocket.

I shut the door. "What's the problem, Officer?"

"We'll get to that, Mr. Tobin," he said. His voice was heavy but uninflected; a monotone, as though he were reading prepared statements. He said, "Turn around and put your hands on the roof of the car."

He was going to frisk me? But it wouldn't be a good idea to argue, so I did as he said. And now I was beginning to comprehend Ronald Cornell's helplessness. When a policeman is your enemy, he has more power than you can deal with. He can do many things to you that skirt the fringes of legality without ever quite falling over the edge, and there is nothing you can do to him at all, nothing at all, that doesn't give him an opening to do even more in return. You cannot beat a policeman, not directly, it's an uneven contest. You can only obey his orders and try to minimize the damage and hope for the best.

I put my hands on the top of my car, and leaned forward on the balls of my feet when he ordered me to do so. He frisked me, quickly and efficiently, and kept nothing but the sheet of paper from my notebook on which I had written down, in brief abbreviations, the questions I wanted to ask Cornell.

"All right, Mr. Tobin, turn around."

I turned around. He was holding the slip of paper, unfolded. He glanced at it, and then looked at me. Snowflakes fell on the paper, and I knew he would not be giving it back to me.

He said, "What is your employment, Mr. Tobin?"

"I don't have any," I said.

"Unemployed? What was your last employment?"

"New York Police Department."

"Yes," he said. He already knew about that. "When did that employment end, Mr. Tobin?"

"Two years ago, a little more."

"Why did it end, Mr. Tobin?" From the way he asked it, he didn't yet know the answer.

"I was dismissed."

"Why?"

"I'd rather not talk about it," I said. "It's a matter of record."

"I'll look it up," he said.

I didn't say anything.

"Mr. Tobin," he said, "since leaving the force, have you applied for or received a license to practice in the State of New York as a private investigator?"

"No."

"Have you *ever* been licensed as a private investigator?"

"No, I haven't."

"Have you ever worked as a private investigator?"

"No."

He smiled thinly at me, and slowly crumpled the piece of paper between his two hands. "Then you have no need for this," he said.

I said nothing.

"And you have no need to talk to any faggots in Brooklyn Heights," he said.

I said nothing.

He said, "Faggots are not in your normal circle of acquaintances, are they, Mr. Tobin?"

"No," I said.

"You're not doing them any favor," he said. "Or yourself. You follow me?"

"Yes," I said.

He studied me for a minute, brooding, and then said, "Are there any questions you'd like to ask me, Mr. Tobin?"

"I don't think so," I said.

"You have no curiosity."

I said nothing.

"I'll tell you anyway," he said. "James Dearborn was murdered by someone he picked up and took home in order to engage in unnatural acts with him. Ronald Cornell tried to kill himself out of grief over his boy friend's death. That's what happened."

He said it forcefully; that either meant he believed it himself or he insisted that I believe it. I said nothing.

He said, "Now that you have no curiosity any more, you don't have any reason to hang around these faggots any more. Do you follow me, Mr. Tobin?"

"I follow you," I said.

"Good," he said. He took my license and registration from his pocket and read them again, slowly. Finally, extending them toward me, he said, "I can always reach you if I need you, isn't that right, Mr. Tobin?"

"That's right," I said. I took the two forms from him.

He nodded heavily at me, and turned away. As he walked back through the snow toward his car, I tucked my license and registration in my coat pocket, and opened my car door. Glancing at Manzoni's car, I saw that his back-seat passenger had twisted around and was looking out the rear window at me, his expression intense.

It was Bruce Maundy.

15

The party was still going on, though more quietly. I could barely hear it from the sidewalk, and it took only one ring to be let in.

It was Remington himself who came out this time, and from his expression as he came down the corridor to open the outer door he wasn't all that happy to see me back again. When he opened the door and I stepped inside I could tell why: the slight scent of marijuana again.

I said, "So I did put a crimp in your party, after all. Did you really think you had to hide the pot till I left?"

"No one wanted to be at more of a disadvantage than necessary," he said. "Is that why you came back, to see if we were doing anything different?"

"No. I came back to talk to you. Seriously, but briefly."

"Privately?"

"Yes."

"We'll go upstairs."

We didn't have to go into the first floor of the apartment, there was a front flight of stairs to take instead. We went up, and Remington led the way down the hall, past the entrance from the rear stairs, and on the familiar route from there to the library.

Henry Koberberg was still in there, alone, reading. He looked up when we walked in, and correctly read displeasure in Stewart Remington's face. "I'm sorry," he said, "did you want this for a conference?" He started to get up.

"That's all right," I said, closing the door. "I'd like you here, too. I think between you, you two know most of what there is to know about my list of suspects."

"We both appear on it," Remington reminded me.

"That complicates things," I admitted, "but doesn't make them impossible. Tell me about Bruce Maundy."

Remington said, "Why?"

"Tell me first."

Remington raised an eyebrow and shrugged. "Rough trade," he said, "with an éclair center."

I turned to Koberg. "Do you agree?"

"Approximately. Bruce has an unfortunately abrasive personality."

"He lives at home with his mother? That makes him the only one on my list who isn't in some sort of on-going living relationship with another man. Does he try to hide the fact of his homosexuality at home?"

Remington laughed for an answer, and Koberg said, "Rabidly. He believes that his mother knows nothing, and he is violent that things should stay that way."

"You say he believes it, about his mother. You think she knows?"

"I've never met the lady. I have no idea how perceptive or intelligent she is."

Remington said, "He probably has it well covered. He lives in two separate worlds, with bulkheads in between, that's all. There are probably half a dozen downstairs like that. No one at home knows, no one at work, no one in the neighborhood. One of them downstairs is married." He turned to Koberg. "You know—Carl."

"You needn't mention names," Koberg said.

"In front of Tobin?"

"Any time. An attorney should know better."

"The things about which I should know better," Remington said in satisfaction, "are legion."

I said, "What was Maundy's relationship with Dearborn?"

Remington said, "They were an item once, long ago. Before Ronnie."

"Why did it end?"

Remington shrugged elaborately. "Why do all Gardens of Eden end? Some sort of snake appeared, I should think."

"You mean Cornell took Dearborn away from him?"

Sounding exasperated with Remington, Koberberg snapped, "Not at all. That was over first."

"They fought, I believe," Remington said. "When one is a black man, and one is in a love affair with a white man, the normal slights and abrasions of love become terribly intensified. Henry could tell you about that."

Koberberg looked offended, as though he would close up entirely and have nothing more to do with the conversation.

I said, "Let's stick to Dearborn and Maundy. What kind of trouble did they have?"

Remington said, "Jamie was not a boy to hide his light under a bushel. But then, he wouldn't be a model otherwise, would he? Jamie loved to be paraded on the arm of his sweetheart; a charming and innocent desire, really. But with Bruce, of course, all had to be secrecy. They couldn't live together, Jamie couldn't visit at Bruce's home, couldn't even *phone* him. Naturally, he would after a while begin to wonder if it was *all* because of Bruce's desire for secrecy, or perhaps just a little bit because of Jamie's skin color."

I said, "Is this a guess on your part, or do you know?"

"I know." His rather heavy-lidded face expressed nostalgic pleasure. He said, "When things were bad between them, Jamie would come to the baths. And there I would be, the fat old spider in the middle of my web. Two or three times he cried on my shoulder, so to speak."

"The break was violent?"

Remington shrugged, smiling. "Everything with Bruce is violent."

Koberberg said, "Shouting only. If you mean physical violence, there was none."

"Only," Remington said, "because Bruce knew just how vain dear Jamie was. To touch Jamie's body in anger would have been to court disaster. Jamie was delicate, but he could be as nasty as a cat if he wanted."

Koberberg said, "In any case, it's all ancient history. It was all over four years ago."

"Was there anyone else for Dearborn between Maundy and Cornell?"

"No," Koberberg said. "Ronnie had been talking about starting a boutique for a long while, but he didn't have enough capital by himself, and he really needed a partner with more flair than he had."

"You should have seen the way he dressed in those days," Remington added.

I nodded; I could guess.

Koberberg said, "I believe Ronnie and Jamie started out as a business partnership, and the other thing happened afterward."

"Propinquity," Remington said lovingly, as though it were a dirty word he'd just looked up in the dictionary. I didn't know how much to believe this leering, oversexed surface of his, it didn't really go with the kind of mind that would be a whole tribe's legal and financial adviser. So it was a mask; but why that particular mask, and what was under it other than the normal shrewdness and sound business sense of the normal businessman?

I said to Koberberg, "You say it was all over with Maundy a long time ago. It hasn't come back to life at all since?"

"I'm sure not," Koberberg said.

"If it had," Remington said, "I'm sure word would have gotten around."

"Who is Maundy connected with now?"

"No one that I know of," Remington said. "I see him at the baths from time to time. Only to wave to, I assure you."

"Why?"

"Why what?"

"Why only to wave to?"

"I prefer a more submissive type," he said delicately and smiled.

Koberberg said, "Bruce doesn't have long affairs, usually. Because of his personality, I suppose, partly. And because he has to keep everything so secret."

"There's no one you can think of since Dearborn?"

"Well—David," Koberberg said, and glanced at Remington. "David Poumon was going around with Bruce for a while, wasn't he?"

"Just for a month or two," Remington said dismissingly. "It wasn't in the stars."

I said, "What was the relationship between Maundy and Dearborn most recently?"

"They were friends," Koberberg said.

"All passion spent," Remington added. "Long, long after the divorce, you might say."

Koberberg said, "Do you mind if I ask you a question?"

"Not at all."

He asked me, "Why this concentration on Bruce? Do you have some specific reason for thinking it was him?"

"He came to my house this morning to threaten me and warn me not to poke into his affairs. When he saw me at the party tonight he left and went to Detective Manzoni to tell him what I was doing. Manzoni just had a talk with me."

Koberberg said, "*Bruce* did that? Are you sure?"

"Yes."

"Security," Remington commented. "He's petrified out of his little wits that you'll go asking his mama questions. He talked to me this afternoon, too, wanted to know what we could do to get rid of you. I suggested he sneak up behind you in the dark with a knife. He wasn't amused."

"I'm not either," I said. "I wish you'd told me before."

"I didn't think his jitters were important."

"Important enough to make trouble for me with Manzoni," I pointed out. "Is there anything else unimportant you're holding back?"

Remington bridled a bit, but then relaxed and nodded. "You're right to be upset," he said. "That was an error of judgment on my part. I frankly haven't been thinking of us as colleagues in this matter, but I suppose I should."

"You should," I said. "What influence have you with Maundy?"

"When he is in a mood to be reasonable, quite a bit, actually. When he is in a mood to be unreasonable, wise men don't answer the phone."

"Can you get him to stop obstructing me?"

"I can try."

"You can point out that if I'm left alone, I won't cause him embarrassment at home, but that if he tries to interfere with me any more, I'll go straight to his house and have a talk with his mother."

Remington gave me a piercing look. "That's not a good bluff," he said, "unless you'd do it."

"I'd do it."

"In that case, it's excellent."

"One thing more," I said, turning to Koberberg. "Everyone I've talked to has had nothing but good things to say about Jamie Dearborn. Except you. Why is that?"

"I am truthful," he said. "Humans generally avoid being unkind about the dead, which is to say, truthful about them. I am truthful."

"And the truth about Dearborn?"

"I had a private nickname for him," he said. "I called him Jamie the Jade."

"What did that mean?"

"If you go downstairs," he said, "you will see any number of thin young things with heavy eye make-up, trying to look like depraved actresses of the silent era. Fake decadence is very modern right now."

"And that was Dearborn?"

"Not at all. Jamie was *truly* decadent, he *was* jaded and bored. The truth is, Bruce Maundy is a nasty brute, and Jamie *loved* being mistreated by him. Not in any physically violent way that would show or affect his good looks, Stew was right about that, but in subtler ways."

"He was a masochist?"

"He was everything. He retired to Ronnie, you know. He was destroying himself, and everyone knew it, and finally he knew it, too. That was why he broke with Bruce. And that was why he went with Ronnie. The way old men sometimes will marry their nurse."

I said, "But from time to time he'd revert to his old ways?"

"Yes."

"With whom?"

"With anyone. Though he preferred to seduce people who were already involved with someone else."

"The equivalent," Remington said, "of the unfaithful wife who sleeps only with married men."

135

"Anyone on my list?" I guessed that Koberberg's partner, Leo Ross, would be one of them.

But the name that Koberberg said, reluctantly, was, "Cary Lane."

That surprised me. Lane's face was unreliable, of course, but I'd thought of him as more innocent than that. I said, "Are you sure?"

"It's common knowledge."

Remington said, "David and Ronnie are about the only ones in the world who don't know."

It was a very narrow world he was talking about there, but I didn't pursue the point. I said, "You're sure David Poumon doesn't know?"

"David doesn't know," Koberberg said flatly. "Cary has been very careful; he cares about David very much. And even if David did know, he wouldn't kill anyone."

"And if he killed anyone," Remington said, "it would be Cary, not Jamie. Besides, he doesn't know, I'm sure of it."

The sexual and emotional ties among these people, which had seemed so simple at first, were starting to complicate themselves. Living in a sub-culture within the normal world, they were more limited for actors from whom to cast the roles in their lives. The same individuals had to play a variety of parts in each other's histories; it became very incestuous after a while.

And which of these threads that I was just beginning to find the ends of would lead me to the killer?

I said, "Then Dearborn was the equivalent of the sub-urban sleep-around wife, is that it? Slept with the husbands of all her friends."

"As many as possible," Remington said dryly.

"Anyone outside my list?"

"God knows," Remington said. "When Ronnie would go

136

off on a trip, Jamie might do just anything."

All at once, everything was turning inside out. I said, "You mean, he might go pick up a stranger somewhere?"

"He could very well," Koberberg said. "It wouldn't be the first time."

"But not take him home," Remington said. "Jamie never did do that."

"You can't say that for sure," Koberberg said to him. "Besides, there's always a first time."

For a few seconds I didn't know what to say next. I had to get used to this idea first, because all of a sudden Manzoni's theory of the Changeable Sailor was a possibility! Cornell had been operating on the false premise that his lover was faithful. But now everything was turned completely around.

Still, did the Changeable Sailor theory explain the attempt on Cornell's life?

Unless that was false, too. Unless Cornell really *had* tried to kill himself, in a state of depression. And was either lying about it, in a panicky attempt to stay out of a mental institution, or had blocked his memory of the truth. It wouldn't be the first time an attempted suicide would have no memory afterward of the attempt.

No, I didn't believe it, not this time. My initial reasoning, when I'd first seen the item in the newspaper, was still valid. And Cornell wouldn't have fallen into despair, if he ever would at all, until after he'd finished his astrology research, which he'd apparently barely begun before being hit on the head and thrown off the roof.

Two killers? The Changeable Sailor killed Dearborn, and someone else tried to kill Cornell. Coincidence? Something resulting out of the first death?

I couldn't do it now, standing here. I had to go away and think things out. I said, "Thank you for talking to me. I'll probably see you both again."

"Any time," Koberberg said, and Remington said, "I'll walk you to the door."

We left the library, and neither of us spoke until we'd reached the first floor. Then I said, "I take it Leo Ross was another of Dearborn's conquests."

"Of course."

"And Ross was less efficient at hiding it from Koberberg than Cary Lane was at hiding it from Poumon."

"Much less. Leo is always inefficient that way. It's part of their relationship, you know."

"Yes. Don't forget to call Maundy."

"I won't."

The aroma of marijuana was stronger than before. "Good night," I said.

"Every night is a good night," he said, and smiled me out.

16

Cornell had a visitor. Cary Lane was sitting in a chair next to the bed, and the bed, the tray, Lane's lap and the floor were covered with open books and sheets of paper. "Jamie was an Aries, too," Lane was saying.

An Aries? And a Jade, according to Koberberg. Faithful, according to Cornell. Faithless, according to Remington and Koberberg, and faithless with this guileless blond young man sitting here in eager participation next to the cuckold.

Was the betrayed member of a homosexual liaison a cuckold?

"But Mars in Aries doesn't lead to compatibility," Cornell said. "Particularly with Mars in conjunction with Venus, and David has it right there." He poked at a sheet of paper.

I said, "Am I interrupting?" It was eleven o'clock, Sunday morning. I hadn't had enough sleep, and I wasn't yet sure what I thought of last night's revelations.

Cornell looked at me with pleasure and hope. "Mr. Tobin! Come in, come in!"

Lane said, "Here, I'll clear off the other chair."

"Don't bother," I said. "I'd rather stand."

"We're making progress," Cornell said excitedly.

Lane was more cautious. "Not really," he said. "We still don't know who the murderer is."

"But we're narrowing it," Cornell said. "We eliminated two." His leg was still up at an angle, but his arms were free to

139

move and the bed was cranked up to a half-sitting position. He was excited to the point where he'd forgotten his physical and legal condition.

I went to the foot of the bed and leaned against it. "You eliminated two? Who?"

"Henry Koberberg and Stew Remington."

"How did you do that?"

Cornell said, "You tell him, Cary."

Lane was shuffling papers and books. "Well, with Stew, he has Venus in Aries. Now that means he'll be compatible with Aries anyway, but it *also* means he'll be compatible with people who have Venus in Pisces—I mean, the most compatible of any Venusian sign—and Jamie had that, too! So even though there might be differences between them sometimes, they'd always have a basic sympathy with one another and wouldn't ever *really* lose their tempers."

Cornell said, "Tell him about the houses."

Did I want to hear about the houses? Or did I want to get on with my own investigation? I had no interest in Cornell's investigation via the occult, but he was for the moment so happy and enthusiastic that I couldn't bring myself to cut him short. So I listened to Lane tell me about the houses.

"Well," Lane said, shuffling more papers, more books, "Aries is the ruler of his second house, and it's in his eighth house now, and that means legacies or somehow making money from the dead. And of course he's representing Ronnie, because of Jamie's death, so that's *that*. Now, there's a suggestion of possible imprisonment in his Leo being in the twelfth house, but without his having done anything *wrong*, necessarily. Having Virgo in the first house, that shows connections with the processes of the law."

Cornell said, "The imprisonment in the twelfth house, that could be *mine*, not necessarily his."

"Oh, yes, of course," Lane said. "Now, Libra in the second house, that's gain through the deceased again; you see, that keeps coming up. So you see, Stew's relationship to all this is perfectly well described, and it doesn't say *anything* about his being violent. Everything is done *to* him."

"Tell him about the Moon," Cornell said.

"Yes, I was going to." More shuffling. "In Stew's *natal* chart, he has the Moon in the eighth house, in adverse aspect to Mars *and* Uranus. Now, that means death, you see, violent or sudden death, with something peculiar about it. Having *both* Mars and Uranus afflicting that way, it's really very dangerous."

"But that means it's done to *him*," Cornell said.

"What it's beginning to look like," Lane said, "there might be danger of more people getting killed."

"Of course," Cornell said, "the Moon business is in the natal chart, so it doesn't necessarily mean right now. But the planets in the particular houses, that describes the current situation."

"And Stew has nothing more to do with it," Lane finished, "than appears on the surface."

"Now, Henry's," Cornell told him.

"Right." A great deal more shuffling. I waited through it, and then Lane said, "Now. Henry has Venus in Leo, that's compatible with Jamie, because of Jamie's Venus in Pisces. That's just overall. Now, the houses, the description of things right now. His Libra, ruler of his third house, is in the eighth. That means trouble because of deaths, and possible false accusations. He's on our suspect list, and it says right here in his horoscope that it's a *false* accusation. You can't get much more specific than that."

"All right," I said.

Cornell, probably knowing I was about to change the sub-

141

ject, quickly said, "There's more."

"Oh, yes, of course," Lane said. "I was just coming to it. His Capricorn in the eleventh house suggests sickness among his friends. But, you see, not through anything he *does*. In fact, the implication is that it saddens him. Then the really interesting one: Aquarius in the twelfth house. Fear of imprisonment caused by close friends. Now! Doesn't *that* say it? Some close friend of Henry's killed Jamie, and created a fear of imprisonment for Henry."

"The imprisonment in Stew's horoscope could be read the same way," Cornell said.

"That's right," Lane said. "I forgot to say that. Now, his Pisces in the first house is trouble through affairs connected with the dead. More of the same, you see. Again, a description of Henry's situation *now*. And it says he's the victim of the circumstances, and not the cause."

Cornell said, "And in his natal chart he has the Moon in the eighth house, too, the same as Stew. With Mars afflicting, meaning violent death."

"Yes," Lane said, "but without Uranus afflicting, so it isn't as dangerous."

"But he has Uranus in the eighth house *with* the Moon, and that means problems arising from deaths."

"Well, that's what he has now," Lane said.

"Yes, but that's the natal chart."

"Well, he has Pluto in the eleventh house in his natal chart," Lane said, "and that means something mysterious in connection with his friendships."

"Nobody *knows* what Pluto means," Cornell said. "It hasn't been studied long enough."

"Well, we know it means things that are hidden and strange. And the eleventh house is friends."

"So it could simply mean being homosexual," Cornell

said. "It doesn't have to have any relevance to right *now*."

This could go on forever. I said, "Excuse me for interrupting, but I have some questions of my own to ask."

"Oh, I'm sorry," Cornell said, very contrite. "I got all caught up. Yes, of course you do. I'm sorry, I shouldn't take your time up with this, I know you don't believe in it."

"I just have other ways of working," I said.

Lane said, "I'll go on and do mine, now. I won't interrupt."

I said to Cornell, "You inherited those things that you and Dearborn owned jointly, is that right?"

"Yes. His money went to his sisters in Nebraska."

"What about you?"

"Me?"

"Who inherits if you die?"

He looked blank, and then said, "My goodness, Jamie does! We did our wills at the same time, leaving everything to each other, except some private things we both had."

"Remington handled it?"

"Yes, naturally."

Lane suddenly said, "*That* isn't right."

We both looked at him, and he was frowning at the papers in his lap. He sensed our sudden silence, and looked up sheepishly to say, "I'm sorry. I just ran across something wrong here."

Cornell said, "In the charts?"

"You have me with Venus in Sagittarius," Lane said. "I'm sorry, I didn't mean to interrupt. I'll just change it here."

Cornell said, "The state I was in, when I was doing those, I'm surprised I got anything right."

"This is the only thing."

They were going to go off again. I said to Cornell, "About your will. What happens if you die without changing it? Is

143

there any contingency in there for Dearborn's death?"

I had his frowning attention again. "I don't remember if there is or not," he said. "I suppose my aunt would inherit, wouldn't she?"

"Your aunt?"

"She's my nearest living relative. She and my uncle brought me up after my mother died. She killed herself."

"Your mother?"

"Because my father deserted her when she got pregnant. With me. She waited till I was born, and then she killed herself."

"So your aunt would inherit. Are you still close to her?"

"Oh, of course. That's where Jerry and I stayed when we went down to Atlanta. I stay there every time I go South."

"She knows about the homosexuality?"

"She doesn't like it, naturally, but she agrees I have to live my own life."

This looked like a dead end, but I followed it through to the finish. "Do you have any idea who inherits from your aunt?"

He smiled, a bit apologetically. "A local school," he said. "It used to be public, and it went private rather than desegregate. A lot of the older people are leaving some or all of their money to it."

"What was your aunt's attitude about your living with a black man, then?"

"She didn't like it, any more than his being a man in the first place."

"Actively disliked?"

"Not really. She didn't try to interfere in my life."

"What about when you went visiting? Ever bring Dearborn with you?"

The apologetic smile returned. "No, that I couldn't do."

"Dearborn knew it?"

"Jamie understood."

Had he? I remembered what I'd been told about Dearborn's reaction to Maundy's craving for secrecy, that he'd found racial meanings in it and had been made upset by them. Had he been unfaithful during Cornell's trips as revenge for Cornell not being able to bring a black man home to Atlanta?

But I had more things I wanted to cover. I said, "Did Dearborn ever do anything to Koberberg that Koberberg might resent?"

"Henry?" He seemed baffled. "But we've already eliminated him, we just told you."

"I'm interested in the way you people behaved within the group," I said. "The relationship between Dearborn and Koberberg could have meaning even if the killing was actually done by somebody else."

He wasn't entirely convinced—the reason I'd given him didn't make much sense, I suppose, but it was better than contradicting his astrology head-on—but he went along with me, saying, "Well, Henry and Jamie didn't really get along very well, but a lot of people have a hard time getting along with Henry, really."

"Do you?"

"Well, I understand him."

"*I* don't get along with him," Cary Lane said, looking up from his papers. "He acts too know-it-all, if you ask me."

I said to Cornell, "Is that what Dearborn thought?"

"Pretty much like that, I guess."

"And how did he act toward Koberberg?"

"I suppose he teased him sometimes."

"Teased him? About what?"

145

"About his appearance, I suppose."

"And his love life," Lane said. "Jamie used to be *merciless* about that. No, it's true, Ronnie, Jamie was really very sweet a lot of the time, but he could be absolutely *vicious* if he put his mind to it."

I said, "And he put his mind to it with Koberberg?"

Lane came very close to giggling. "Well, there's just something so *stuffed shirt* about Henry. I suppose Jamie couldn't help *tweaking* him sometimes."

"And how would Koberberg react?"

Lane said, "Oh, he used to make believe Jamie was beneath contempt, you know. Very Queen Victoria, 'We are not amused,' that sort of thing." The quote was done in an excellent imitation of Henry Koberberg's voice.

"Koberberg never fought back?"

"Well, what could he *do*, actually?" Lane asked.

"I don't know. That's why I'm asking what he did."

Cornell said, "He never did anything. And it really wasn't that much, just sometimes at parties or wherever. And Henry really isn't a violent man, you know. Aside from what the stars say."

"What about Leo Ross? Would he defend Koberberg?"

"Oh, Leo never takes anything seriously," Cornell said. Lane had gone back to his papers. Cornell said, "Leo likes things to be light and amusing. When it would start to get serious, Leo would just go away. In anything."

"How did he and Dearborn get along?"

"Leo? Oh, they got along fine. They both liked things to be bright and pleasant."

"Was either of them a militant?"

"You mean in the race thing? Good Lord, no. They both just took things as they came. Leo still does, of course. But Jamie didn't want to get involved in that kind of thing either."

Lane, his voice a little odd, said, "Ronnie?" He was frowning at the papers in his lap.

Cornell looked over at him. "What's the matter?"

"Look up some things for me," Lane said, his voice still strange. "Just to check what I have over here."

"You want me to use this book?"

I said, "I don't have much more to talk about. Couldn't this wait?"

Lane, when he looked at me, was obviously both frightened and upset. "Please, Mitch," he said. "This is important, I think. And it won't take long, I promise it won't."

"All right," I said. There was nothing to be gained by antagonizing them, and I doubted I'd be able to keep Cornell's attention even if I tried at this point. So I leaned on the foot of the bed, and watched, and listened.

Lane said, reading from his papers, "Natal chart. Mars in the third house, afflicted by Neptune."

"Afflicted by Neptune?" Cornell was leafing through a fat book with a faded white cover. A dozen strips of paper marked places in it. "Here," he said. "Suicidal tendencies. Violent tendencies."

"Moon in the seventh house, afflicted by Saturn and Uranus."

"Uhh—" Leafing pages. "Saturn adverse; sorrow through partnerships, marriage, unions. Uranus adverse; estrangement, unexpected attacks, odd experiences in connection with unions."

"Death of partner?" Lane asked.

"Oh, yes. Generally, if bad aspected."

"Saturn in the seventh."

"Afflicted?"

"Yes."

"Death of partner again. Treachery. Incompatibil-

147

ity. Coldness in partner."

"Uranus in the eighth, afflicted."

"Worry about legacies. Unexpected problems arising from deaths. Extraordinary or violent death." Solemn-eyed, Cornell said, "Is this you?"

"Just listen. Now, in the progressed chart. Libra, ruler of first, in twelfth."

"Ruler of first in twelfth." Another section of the book. "Fear of imprisonment. Secret unhappiness."

"Taurus, ruler of eighth, in seventh, afflicted."

"Let's see." He read, then looked up to stare at Lane, stare at me, then look at the book again. "Death of partner. Danger of death by suicide or violence. Good Lord, Cary!"

"There's more. Virgo, ruler of the twelfth house, in eleventh."

"Unfortunate enterprises. Deceitful friends and great disappointments." Cornell looked at him again. "This is you, isn't it?"

"I'm doing David's now," he said. "Moon in the eighth house, natal chart." He looked over at Cornell. "Stew and Henry both had that, too."

"Afflicted?"

"Neptune."

"That's—wait just a minute. Death by treachery, or water, or drugs, or some ob—"

"Oh, my God!" Lane's plastic face looked shrunken, hollow, as though the real skull inside it had been removed and it was slowly collapsing in on itself.

Were they actually going to drive themselves into hysterics with this? I came close to saying something, interrupting, trying to break the spell, but I had the feeling an insertion from me just now would do more harm than good, so I simply waited to see where all this would wind up.

But didn't horoscopes always say cheerful things, like, "You are kind, witty, of quick intelligence and interested in astrology" and so on? What was all this death? What were these books?

Lane, meantime, was saying, "Mars in the eighth, afflicted." His nervousness was making him jumble his words; they bumped and ricocheted off one another.

Cornell said, "Still in the natal chart?"

"Yes, of course!" Sudden panicky rage. "What else would it be?"

Cornell didn't take offense, luckily. He bent to his books and said, "Sudden or violent death. Loss of legacy. Loss of money through partner. In a watery sign?"

"What? Oh! No, in Aries. An airy sign."

"Death by mental afflictions or air accidents." Cornell looked at Lane again and said, very low, "Mental afflictions."

"Yes, I know. Saturn in the eleventh, afflicted."

"Saturn in the eleventh. False friends. A cardinal sign?"

"Yes, Cancer."

"Emphasizes the reading. Is that all for the natal?"

"Yes."

"It could be any time in his life."

"It's talking about the *end* of his life, Ronnie!"

"Yes, but that could be any time."

"*My* chart says I lose my partner *now.*"

"It could be any time in the next few weeks," Cornell said. "And it isn't predetermined anyway, it's simply the *leaning.*"

"But everything—Wait, let me see what the progressed—" He bent over the papers and his own books, turning pages, taking notes, losing some of his incipient hysteria in his absorption with the work.

Cornell said to me, "This will take a minute or two, Mr.

149

Tobin. I'm sorry. But if it's true—"

"If what is true?"

"Well, you can never be absolutely sure," he said, "but it sounds as though David is going to die."

"Please!" Lane said, his head still bowed over the books and papers. He was trembling like a nervous dog.

I said, "Could it mean he'll be arrested?" Whatever happened, I wanted them both calmer than this.

"It could mean all sorts—"

The door opened. Lane kept studying, but Cornell and I both turned our heads to look, and saw Detective Manzoni come into the room.

17

Manzoni said, "Mr. Tobin, you're a damn fool."

I didn't say anything; unfortunately, Cornell did. "It isn't Mr. Tobin's fault, Mr. Manzoni," he said. "I'm the one who hired him to help—"

"You *hired* him?"

"Yes, of course." He didn't get it, he didn't know why he should keep his mouth shut. But there was no reason why he should have known any better. He said, "Mr. Tobin wouldn't be involved in all this if it wasn't for me, so there's no reason to—"

"Just a minute. You. You! Wake up!"

He meant Lane, who finally sprang his head up from the books and papers, looking blank and frightened. "What? What?"

"What's your name, is it Lane?"

"What? Yes!"

"All right, Lane, I want you to listen to something." The door was still open and the uniformed patrolman was standing there; Manzoni was collecting witnesses from all over. He said to Cornell, "Now, tell me what Mr. Tobin's doing here."

Cornell had belatedly realized he shouldn't be talking, and now, instead of answering, he glanced uncertainly at me.

Manzoni snapped, "Never mind looking at him now! Tell me again why he's here. And you," to Lane. "You pay attention."

"But this is important!" Lane cried. "You don't under—"

"You shut up, Lane. It's Ronnie I want to hear from. Well, Ronnie?"

"Go ahead," I said. There was nothing to be gained by stalling at this point.

Cornell said, in a subdued voice, "I hired him to help me find Jamie's murderer." And then, more fiercely, "Because the police wouldn't even *try!* Meaning *you,* Mr. Manzoni! Go ahead and remember that, too, Cary!"

Manzoni looked at me, and if he felt any satisfaction, I couldn't see it in his face. "I warned you last night, Mr. Tobin," he said. "You know what this is, you being here like this?"

"A felony," I said. "Working without a private investigator's license." Saying it for Cornell's benefit.

"More than that," he said. "It's a personal insult directed at me. You're standing there saying I don't know how to do my job."

"You don't," I said. Not loudly, not argumentatively. He didn't, and I knew he didn't, and I said it.

He blinked. But then he said, "I looked up your history this morning, Mr. Tobin. There's some people I might listen to when they'd tell me I didn't know my job. You aren't one of them."

"I know."

Lane, who had gone back to his books and papers, suddenly cried, "Here it is! Ronnie, here it is!"

Manzoni glared at him, annoyed at the interruption. "What the hell is this?"

Lane shouted, "Ruler of the eighth in the fourth, and ruler of the twelfth in the eighth!"

"I told you before to shut up," Manzoni said angrily. "One more outburst and I'll have you put out of here."

Lane didn't say anything else, but not because of Manzoni's threat. He was perched on the edge of his chair, anxious, terrified, even bouncing slightly as he watched Cornell leaf through the pages of one of the books.

Manzoni turned back to me. In relief, I think; I had attitudes and reactions he could understand. He said, "It's for the insult, Mr. Tobin, and for no other reason. You could practice anything you wanted without a license, and I wouldn't worry about it very much. But it's the insult that offends me."

I said, "There's no doubt in your mind? This man in the bed here has suffered a lot already. Are you sure you aren't making him suffer even more than he has to—are you *sure?*"

"This what in the bed?"

"Faggot," I said. "Human being."

"You're also a social worker without a license, is that it?"

"You don't think you're doing your job right any more than I do. You *know* you're railroading Cornell."

"That's a lie!" He was stung now, and I became aware for the first time of the heavy implacability of his anger. And how easily Cornell or any of the fragile blossoms around Jamie Dearborn could all unwittingly hit that button in his head. Manzoni would be a frightening enemy because he was such an accomplished liar when lying to himself.

"You do know it," I said, quietly insisting. I had no real hope of breaking through, but perhaps if I was quiet enough, something of what I said might seep through the stone wall of his resistance, like water into a basement.

Where I would have preferred to be right now.

Cornell read softly, "Death of parents, danger from falling or falling objects. Eighth house; an unsatisfactory finish, many troubles, secret enemies die, problems with inheritance."

"It's now," Lane said. Pushing papers and books from his lap to the floor, he rose like a robot and stared blindly around. "It's now."

Manzoni said heavily, "What the hell is all this?"

I said, "Astrology. They believe in astrology."

"Someone's going to kill David," Lane said, very quietly. He stared at me. "Mitch? You'll have to go help him!"

"That's enough of that," Manzoni said. "Your friend Mitch is coming along with me. He has a statement to make."

"Mitch, you *have* to go!"

"I'm sorry," I said. "I'll have to go with Detective Manzoni. You go on home and call—"

"That's all, Mr. Tobin," Manzoni said. "Come along." He extended a hand toward my elbow, without quite touching it. His face and manner said, *Don't force me to use physical means, because I will enjoy using them.*

"Mitch!"

"Call Remington," I told him, and started toward the door. "He'll help you," I said.

He called my name again; his voice was full of disbelief that I would walk away from him when his stars said there was trouble.

I already had trouble.

Manzoni and I left the hospital.

18

There was a time in this country when it was easier than it is now for a police officer to hold a citizen for an extended period of time without charging him with any particular offense or permitting him any phone calls or other contact with the outside world. Back when confessions were worth something in court, it was standard operating procedure in some kinds of cases to keep a suspect for days, for a week or more, and hammer at him with teams of detectives in relays, moving him from precinct to precinct if necessary to keep him away from his lawyers and family until his resistance was finally broken down and he was prepared to trade away a confession that might cost his life for a chance at eight hours of uninterrupted sleep.

A lot has changed in recent years. The confession means a lot less than it used to, and the more abrasive police techniques have been softened here and there. But that doesn't mean the police are, as the editorial writers like to claim, "handcuffed." Far from it. They still have more weapons in their arsenal than the private citizen has in his.

One of the most effective of those weapons is the simplest: red tape. The first two hours I was at Manzoni's precinct house were spent in the droning process of filling out forms. I knew the technique, I'd used it myself more than once when I was on the force, but it was effective just the same. I sat there in that overheated office—snow was falling lazily again outside the second-story windows, having stopped for several hours this morning—and a bored, lazy uniformed patrolman sat at a typewriter and asked me questions and slowly pecked the answers onto form after form. I knew most of this paper was for no reason at all, that once I was gone the forms would all—or most of them—be thrown in the garbage, but I hadn't been given any choice. So I answered the questions, and tried not to look at my watch every five minutes, and tried to find something to occupy my attention while the minutes and the seconds crept slowly by.

I hate to be in a police station these days; it brings back too much of the past, when I was a different person living a different life. Other individuals in my current position might help to push the time by a little faster by becoming absorbed in the flow and movement of the bullpen, the large open room full of battered wooden desks where the detective squad worked, and where I was now being given the stall treatment. Others might enjoy watching the plainclothesmen come in, sit at their desks, answer phones, drink paper cups of water from the water cooler in the far corner, peck out reports on typewriters at the tables along the wall where my typist and I were sitting, occasionally spend time talking with visitors who had come in voluntarily or been brought upstairs by uniformed patrolmen; all the quiet natural life of every bullpen in every precinct house in the city. Others in my position might distract their minds with that, but I couldn't. The movement around me was the worst torture of all; for me, the endless pointless questions and the slow dragged-out filling-in of blanks on useless forms was the distraction.

After an hour there was a change of typists, a second uniformed man taking the place of the first. The second one was, if anything, slower than the first, and more impersonal. He also spent longer away at the filing cabinets, finding other forms to fill out.

And through all that time, I never once saw Manzoni. He had brought me up here, deposited me in this chair, gone across the room to talk briefly with the first of my typists, and had then gone into the office marked, in black lettering on opaque glass, CAPTAIN OF DETECTIVES. I hadn't seen him since.

Nor did I see him now. It was a different plainclothesman who came over at last and said to typist number two, "When you're finished with him, take him down to room 214."

"Right."

The plainclothesman gave me a flat incurious look and walked away.

There were no more forms. The typist slowly finished the one he was working on, double-checked all the items with me —as usual, most of the items being the same on every form— and then at last got to his feet and said, "Come on."

We left the bullpen and went down the hall together, not speaking. The hall was wide and high-ceilinged, with an old wooden floor and with large light globes hanging down at intervals from the paint-peeling ceiling. The walls were painted dark green to a height of four feet, and then light green above that. They were scratched in many places. The paint peeling from the ceiling was a cream color, darkened by age.

Room 214 contained a gray metal desk, a swivel chair behind the desk, a wooden chair with slatted back beside the desk, a black linoleum floor, a gray metal filing cabinet, a round dark green metal wastebasket, a cork bulletin board on the wall beside the desk, gray walls, once-white ceiling, and a wide window covered with a venetian blind.

"Wait here," the typist said, and closed the door, and went away.

The room was empty, except for me. There was nothing on the bulletin board, except two slightly rusty thumb tacks. I went over to the window and separated two venetian blind slats and looked out at the gray bricks of an air shaft. I opened the drawers of the filing cabinet, and they were empty. I opened the drawers of the desk: pencils, ballpoint pens, sheets of blank paper, paper clips, rubber bands, a half-used pack of matches, envelopes of various sizes. Not enough of anything, and nothing of a personal nature.

There was one slat missing from the back of the wooden chair.

I went back to the window, opened the blinds, raised them. I stood there looking out at the wall awhile, then walked around the room, then went back and leaned against the high window sill and looked at the room awhile.

The light source was—other than the window, which was very dirty—a fluorescent light fixture hanging from the ceiling. A long one, with the kind of thing across the fluorescent tubes that looks like the cross-hatched interior of an egg carton. The fixture was obviously a recent addition to the room; more recent, in any case, than the rest of the room. Some money had been spent on modernization, and the result was a fluorescent light in an interrogation room.

Despite myself, I found my mind turning to the precinct building I had worked out of—the age of it, the feel and look and smell of it, the odd touches of modernization here and there as dribs of money had become available. And Jock, who had found most things funny, would have laughed at a fluorescent light in a room like this. If I hadn't killed him.

I was there forty-five minutes, and I was pacing back and forth, trying to control nerves and rage, when the door at last opened and two people I didn't know walked in. Both were in civilian clothes, and one carried a stenographer's notebook.

He was slender, somewhat shabbily dressed, and had a small neat head and wore large black-framed eyeglasses. The other one, a stocky man of about forty, wore a wrinkled brown suit, the jacket open over a wrinkled white shirt and a wrinkled narrow dark brown tie. I looked at him, and found myself wondering what Ronald Cornell would think of his clothing, and what this man would think of Ronald Cornell's clothing, and with that thought I managed to regain control of myself and not do anything stupid.

I had been very close to doing something stupid. Screaming, or hitting somebody, or trying to leave.

The brown-suited man said to me, "Sit down, Mr. Tobin," gesturing at the wooden chair beside the desk. Then he looked around and said, "No other chair?"

"I'll get one, sir," the male stenographer said, and left again.

I hadn't moved. The brown-suited man looked at me without pleasure and said, "I'd prefer it if you'd sit."

There was nothing to be gained by antagonizing him. I sat down, and he came around me and sat at the desk. He spent a minute or two opening and closing drawers, not so much looking for anything in particular as just settling in, making himself at home, the way a dog circles three or four times before lying down.

He did remove a pencil from the middle drawer, to play with, and played with it. Watching his fingers play with the pencil, he said, as one harassed human being to another, "I don't know why they don't put a phone in here."

I didn't say anything.

"But you know how it is," he said, and glanced at me. "You were on the force, weren't you?"

I nodded, and looked away from him at the window. Neither of us said anything further.

The stenographer finally came back, carrying another wooden chair, this one with all its slats. He put it in the corner behind me, and sat down. "Ready, sir."

"Fine." He began tapping the eraser end of the pencil on the desk, thinking about things; then said to the stenographer, "Shut those blinds, will you? I hate that wall out there."

"Yes, sir."

"I don't know who keeps opening those things."

Movement, shuffling, time-killing.

The man at the desk said to me, "We want you to make a statement. You don't have to if you don't want. You can request legal counsel if you want, you can make a phone call if you want."

It was three hours since I'd been brought to the precinct, and now I'd been given the options the law guarantees me. The Supreme Court has still left slack in the line.

I said, "I don't want to make a statement. I don't want legal counsel. I don't want to make a phone call."

He studied me neutrally. "That's up to you, of course. We would like you to answer some questions, and before you do you have the right—"

"I don't intend to answer any questions," I said.

He frowned. "Mr. Tobin, up to this point you've been cooperative. That will have some weight, of course, as to whether or not you're ultimately charged. You haven't been charged as yet, and now—"

"The time has come," I said.

The frown deepened. "What time, Mr. Tobin?"

"The time to shit or get off the pot," I said.

"Mr. Tobin, a record is being made of this conversation. Certain language should—"

"Then let the record show," I said, "that I have been held against my will for three hours before being apprised of my rights. Let the record—"

"Against your will? Mr. Tobin, our workload here is such—"

"Complain to Centre Street, I don't do your financing. Let the record show that I have, at"—I checked my watch—"twenty minutes to five in the afternoon on Sunday, the eighteenth of January, requested that I be either charged with a crime or released."

"Mr. Tobin," he said, "I'm a little surprised at your attitude. You *are* guilty of a felony. You need a break around here. Whether you are charged with that felony or not is at our discretion."

"Then choose," I said. "Either charge me or release me. Now. I played your game for three hours, and now I don't want to play any more."

"Game? Mr. Tobin, your choice of language—"

"As you pointed out," I said, "before the record started to be taken, I used to be on the force. So I know this game, I've played it myself from your side, I know all about it."

"Mr. Tobin, what you did when you were on the—"

"Was from time to time exactly what you're doing now. Punishment on the spot. When you've got somebody, and you don't like him, but for one reason or another you don't want to go through the process of arrest and trial, you just sweat him awhile, make him remember you."

"Your interpretation of events is up to you," he said. "But I'll point out that I've never seen you before, that you were guilty of a felony, that there are witnesses to that felony, and that it is in my power to give you a break."

"You mean, give Manzoni a break."

"If you mean the arresting officer, Mr. Tobin, you are making no sense."

"The felony we keep talking about," I said, "is operating

as a private investigator without a license from the State of New York. You couldn't charge me on that without Detective Manzoni's handling of a couple of recent cases being eventually brought up in court. I might be jailed for a year or two, though I'd most likely just be fined. Nothing official would be done to Manzoni, but his record would from then on have a little messy spot in it, a little spot that suggested he couldn't be relied on one hundred percent. Manzoni would have seen his last promotion, and there isn't one of us in this building that doesn't know it. If you're going to give me the break you're so proud of, do it now. If you're going to give Detective Manzoni a black eye, do *that* now. Charge me or release me, but do it now."

He had grown a little red during my speech, not from embarrassment but from anger, and now he said, "The last thing you want to do, fellow, is give me orders."

I looked at my watch again. "In sixty seconds I'm leaving this room. You can do what you want about it."

He started to say something angry, but suddenly caught himself and gave me a bleak smile instead. "All right, Mr. Tobin," he said. "You used to be in the system, you know how it works. Fred, stop taking notes."

"Yes, sir."

"You can leave." But that was said to the stenographer, not to me.

We both waited while he got to his feet, closed his notebook, put his pencil away in his shirt pocket, and picked up his chair. He left, carrying the chair out of the room with him, and shut the door.

The detective said, "All right, Tobin, what's the problem?"

"No problem," I said. "I'll go now."

"Don't hard-nose me," he said. "What's Manzoni into?"

"Nothing that would interest a fellow officer."

"Forget that. If Manzoni's heading for trouble, the captain wants to know about it."

I looked at him. "You're the funnel?" It happened that way, in some precincts: a captain who neither liked nor trusted his men found one of them to spy on the others for him. A funnel, with the wide end in the bullpen and the narrow end in the captain's ear.

He said, reasonably, "What does it matter to you, Tobin? You don't have any reason to love Manzoni."

And yet I still had the bullpen mentality; I automatically sided with Manzoni against the captain's stooge. I said, "I don't have any reason to love anybody around here."

"You won't level with me? Just the two of us, no witnesses, off the record."

I got to my feet. "Good-bye," I said.

"You may want a friend some day," he said.

"I wouldn't want it to be you," I said, and left the little office. I shut the door behind me.

19

Manzoni himself was coming down the corridor toward me, and I was so absorbed in my own affairs, and my reactions to the smell of precinct politics I'd just been given a whiff of, that I didn't notice at first that he looked urgent and intense and worried. I braced myself for trouble from him, and it wasn't until he spoke that I realized the trouble was his this time, and not mine.

He said, "Forget all that." As though we'd already been having a conversation. His speed and intensity were the signs of the disaster that had overtaken him, whatever it was. He said, "Are you done in there?" As though it had been a physical examination at a doctor's office; in any case, something I'd done on my own, that he'd had nothing to do with.

I said, "What now?"

"I want to talk to you. Is Carpenter still in there?" He headed for the room I'd just left. Looking back at me, he said, with irritation, "Come on, will you?" As though we were to stop playing now, something serious had come up.

Just as he reached for the doorknob—and I was trying to make up my mind whether to stick around for this or not—the door opened and Carpenter came out. He looked flustered when he saw Manzoni, and more so when he saw me. He must have thought I'd told Manzoni about him, or in any case, intended to. I didn't; what they did to each other in here made no difference to me.

But Carpenter didn't know that. "Hi, Aldo," he said, and his nervousness was so intense that if Manzoni hadn't already been caught up in this other thing, he would have understood it all right then and there, without being told by anybody. But Manzoni could see nothing right now other than his own problems, and he nodded a distracted greeting, pushed past Carpenter into the room, and gestured through the doorway irritably for me to follow.

Carpenter tried to catch my eye, to warn me to keep my mouth shut, but I wouldn't let it be caught. I had decided I wanted to know what had happened that had so disturbed Manzoni, so I, too, stepped past Carpenter and went back into the little office, and Manzoni shut the door in Carpenter's face.

I said, "What is it?"

Neither of us contemplated sitting down. Manzoni paced halfway to the window, turned back, gave me a tightly anguished look, said, "David Poumon's dead."

My immediate reaction was, *Cary Lane did it, to make the prophesy come true.* Only after that did I think, *It came true!*

Manzoni had pulled a pack of cigarettes from his pocket, and was nervously poking a finger into it, trying to get at one of the last remaining cigarettes. "But it's all right," he said. "We got him."

"You got who?"

"The one who did it. Another spade faggot, named Leo Ross. You've met him."

That's astonishing, I thought. I said, "How was he gotten?"

"He made a stupid mistake. He locked himself on the roof."

"I don't follow you."

"Tobin, what the hell does it matter how this all happened? The point is, Poumon's dead."

"You're going to fit Ross for the Dearborn killing, too?"

"Fit him?"

"I don't mean frame. Do you think he's it?"

Manzoni shrugged. With obvious reluctance, he said, "He probably is. We'll have to talk to him when they bring him in."

I said, "And Cornell, too?"

He didn't quite meet my eye. "We'll look into that, too."

"Now that there's been another death. Do you want Cornell to pay you what he was going to pay me, or will your city salary be enough?"

His anger was mostly defensive. "I followed my opinion," he said, meeting my eye now, glaring at me. "I acted about the facts the way I read them."

"The sad thing is," I said, "you half-believe that. Within a week you'll believe it all the way. What do you want with me now, Manzoni? I'm tired, I want to go home."

"What the other one said at the hospital," he said, reluctant, hesitating. "You know, Lane."

"When he said Poumon would be killed?"

"It was supposed to be astrology!" he burst out peevishly, as though *he* were the one being treated unfairly. "Who'd pay any attention to that?"

I didn't want to give Manzoni the benefit of any doubts, I disliked him too much for that, but I couldn't help putting myself in his place and wondering how I would have reacted under the same circumstances. One murder, one attempted murder. Somebody deeply involved in the case says there'll be a third, and gives the name of the victim. When asked the source of his information, he says astrology. (Or a Tarot deck. Or palmistry. Or ESP. Or the I Ching. Or a dream. Or whatever.) What would I do?

I would talk with him. I would not place credence in his source, but I would talk with him, I would try to find out if

166

other things in the environment of the murder had given him hints he didn't fully understand and had unconsciously converted to a medium he did understand; in this case, astrology. I might eventually turn away, saying there was nothing in it, just as Manzoni had done, but first I would have talked with him. Which Manzoni had not done.

But Manzoni's question to me just now had not required an answer, and so I gave it none. He rushed on, saying, "Why obscure the issue? That doesn't have to come up at all. You're out of it, I'm out of it, Cornell is out of it, we've got the killer, so why drag in anything else?"

I said, "You're telling me you don't want me to mention to anybody that you were warned Poumon would be killed."

"He said it was astrology!"

"Whatever he said it was, you don't want me to mention it."

His mouth moved, his hands moved, as though he would present arguments; at last he just dropped his hands to his sides, shrugged, and said, "That's right."

"Manzoni," I said, "you're the worst judge of human nature I ever met in my life. *I'm* not going to mention *anything* about this mess to *anybody*. I'm going home, and I'm going to stay there. But Ronald Cornell and Cary Lane are going to crucify you; those two faggots, as you love to call them, are going to nail you to the cross, and I couldn't be happier about it."

"You bastard, what right have you got to—"

"No right at all. I've seen cops like you before, Manzoni, I worked with some in the old days and I could never get used to them. Self-righteousness instead of brains. You're a threat to everybody in the world who isn't named Manzoni, and it's a rare treat to see one of you birds become at last a threat to himself. Good-bye," I said, and left, and went home.

20

Kate wanted me to see Cornell again, but there was no point to it, so I didn't do it. I was still very surprised that it had turned out to be Leo Ross, but whoever it had turned out to be I wasn't the one who'd found him, so I rated no payment. Cornell was out from under the Manzoni threat, Ross was in jail, I wasn't going to be hassled for practicing without a license after all, and there was nothing left to be done. The whole thing was finished, as far as I was concerned. That evening, and again the next morning, I went back to work in the basement.

Except it wasn't finished.

Kate came downstairs about three o'clock the next afternoon, Monday, to tell me Henry Koberberg was in the living room and wanted to talk to me.

I should have known he'd be along. He wasn't a stupid man, far from it; it was only inevitable that he would come to me.

Because it wasn't Leo Ross. I knew damn well it wasn't Leo Ross. That amiable, clever man hadn't killed anybody, and I knew it. And I knew why he'd been framed, and I knew why Poumon had been killed, and I absolutely knew who'd done it all: the killings, the attack on Cornell, the framing of Ross, everything. I didn't know the exact details of motive for the original murder of Jamie Dearborn, but everything else I knew.

I'd known it from the instant I'd heard Poumon was really

168

dead. I'd known it, and I'd pushed the knowledge down under the surface of my thoughts, because I didn't have one item of proof. I had nothing but personalities and relationships and some understanding of needs. Not enough. Not enough for me to say a name to Manzoni, so I'd pushed it under instead. I suppose I'd thought, down in the level under conscious thought, that the truth would out somehow anyway. It wasn't likely Manzoni would be staying in charge of the case much longer, and the next man wouldn't have any vested interest in obsolete theories to keep him from seeing the truth.

Of course, back when I'd read about Cornell's accident in the newspaper I'd made the same easy assumptions, and it hadn't quite worked out that way.

And here was Koberg, calling me to come back to the surface once again. I stood leaning on the shovel, looking at Kate, and she stood on the third step from the bottom, waiting for me. I considered the arguments I might try, and knew they were no good. I shook my head, and put the shovel down, and went upstairs.

As usual, I had to wash first. When I went into the living room, Koberg was sitting in the chair just to the right of the door. He was wearing his topcoat; his hat was in his lap. He had the stunned look I've seen sometimes on the faces of survivors of bad automobile accidents, as though the mind hasn't yet moved past the instant of the impact, is still back there, stuck in a cleft in time, while the body has come along through the minutes without it.

He looked at me and said, "He's innocent."

"I know," I said. "Bruce Maundy did it."

He blinked, and on the other side of the blink his face was subtly different; his mind, jolted out of the cleft way back in yesterday, had suddenly rejoined him. He said, "Bruce? Are you sure?"

169

I said, "I have no proof. I have no way of getting proof."

"The police could," he said, "if they'd bother to look."

"I'm not well connected with that precinct," I said. "They'd listen to you before they'd listen to me."

"Manzoni won't listen to anyone," he said.

I said, "Manzoni? He's still in charge?"

"Of course. Why wouldn't he be?"

"Haven't Lane and Cornell made any statements?"

"Cary is at my place. He collapsed after he found the body. I've been trying to take care of him."

To ward off, I suppose, his own collapse. I said, "What about Cornell?"

"I really don't know. Ronnie's still at the hospital, naturally. Statements about what?"

Instead of answering him, I said, "Isn't there any kind of on-going police investigation?"

"Why should there be? They have their man," he said bitterly.

"Aren't they interested in motive? In proofs?"

"They have Leo, that's all the proof they seem to need. Good heavens, man, he's black *and* he's queer! What do you expect from the police department?"

I said, "Then I don't know what to say. You could try talking to Manzoni, he might be a little more accessible now that his first theories have been proved wrong."

He shook his head. He said, "I'm not entirely sure why you're trying to evade the responsibility of this, but you know you aren't being honest with me. Detective Manzoni is not accessible to me, nor will he ever be."

I said, "But I don't have any *proof,* don't you see that? I know it was Maundy, I know why he did it, but I can't prove any of it."

"Shouldn't you be out looking for proof?" he asked me.

"Why? You say it's my responsibility. *Why* is it my responsibility?"

"Because there's no one else to do it," he said. "The only man who can do the job always has the responsibility to do it."

Operating without a license again. I shook my head, angry at myself, at Koberberg, at Maundy, at Manzoni, at the whole world. I said, "Tell me Ross's story."

Ross's story was a simple one, though in the telling, complex. He had received a phone call from someone with a disguised voice, saying he had proof that *Koberberg* was the murderer of Jamie Dearborn, and offering to sell the proof for a hundred dollars. (Such an incredibly small amount!) He had arranged to meet Ross on the roof of the building housing Lane and Poumon's apartment. Their building, it seemed, was more of an apartment house, six stories high and with twenty-four tenants. Ross recognized the address, of course, but didn't know yet what it meant.

In any case, he agreed to the meeting, and he went to it armed with a length of pipe wrapped with a woman's stocking, for self-defense. He took the elevator at the apartment building to the top floor, went up the last flight of stairs to the roof, and stepped out to find the roof empty. He propped the door open and walked around the roof, looking over the edge here and there, and when he got back to the door, it was shut and locked.

He shouted, of course, but no one heard him. This was just around four the previous afternoon, Sunday, when the windless snowfall had recently started up again. A snow like that muffles sounds.

The law requires a fire escape from the roof, but in some parts of the city waves of burglaries have led building owners to remove the top flight of fire escapes, and police—as anxious as anyone to see the number of burglaries lowered—tend not to notice the violation. That had happened here, and there was no longer any way for Ross to get off the roof.

He finally decided the only thing to do was wait for either Lane or Poumon to enter or leave the building, and he stayed at the front edge of the roof to watch for them. He planned to drop the length of pipe when he saw them, to attract their attention. Then he would shout and wave his arms, they would see him, they would rescue him.

Of course, he wasn't looking straight down the front of the building the whole time. It was cold up there, and it was snowing, and he had to move around to keep himself a bit warm. It is also very hard, after a while, to go on staring indefinitely at one spot, no matter what the situation.

So he missed Lane. Of course, Lane had been hurrying home, rushing from the hospital as a result of the warning he'd seen in the horoscopes, and had run directly from the cab under the canopy and into the building.

While Ross continued to stand around on the roof, feeling more and more like a fool and wondering if he should take the chance of dropping one flight to the beginning of the fire escape—the ground, sixty feet away, deterred him—Lane took the elevator to his fifth-floor apartment, searched it for Poumon, saw a bedroom window standing open, knew it shouldn't be open in such cold weather, and looked out, to see Poumon's body lying in the middle of the building's trash cans below.

It was Lane who called the police. It was the police who eventually went up on the roof and found Ross. And when they searched him, they found the length of pipe in his pocket. He told his story, but it wasn't believed.

I said, "The police believe Ross took Poumon to the roof and threw him off from there?"

"Yes."

"Why? With Poumon already on the fifth floor, why do they think Ross took him up two flights more?"

"You were a policeman," Koberberg said. "You know the phrase *modus operandi*. Ronnie was dragged to the roof and thrown off, and so David must have been as well."

"Very sloppy thinking," I said. I was pacing the floor, trying to find the handle. "There might be something on the window sill," I said. "Something in the apartment somewhere. But it would take professionals to find out."

"You're a professional," Koberberg said.

I stopped and looked at him and shook my head. "There are no Renaissance men any more," I told him. "I was a professional badge-carrier at one time, no more and no less. What we need in that apartment is professionals in the police sciences. People who put a thread under a microscope and tell you what color and make of coat it came from. That isn't my field, and it never was."

"I see. I'm sorry, yes, you're absolutely right. I think of a policeman as someone with all the police skills combined in one head."

"It doesn't happen," I said.

"So what is needed is to give the police department some incentive to do its own investigation." He peered at me. "What was it that convinced you Bruce was guilty?"

"When I heard that Poumon had been killed. Maundy did it to distract Manzoni."

"Distract? I don't follow."

I said, "All right, from the beginning. All of you people share an interest in astrology, that's number one."

"Mine is more critical than the others," he said mildly. "I consider astrology very interesting, but not yet proven."

"In any event, you're involved in it. So are all the others, including Bruce Maundy. He even had something to say about it when he came here to warn me off the other day."

Koberberg nodded. "All right. Point number one accepted."

I said, "The killer knew Cornell was trying to use astrology to solve the murder. You all knew that, and the killer had to see the stuff on Cornell's desk when he tried to kill *him*."

"Naturally."

"So he'd check into it himself, wouldn't he? Run his own horoscope, look in all the books, just to find out if there was something dangerous to him in there or not."

"I suppose we all did that," Koberberg said. "Leo and I did. We both found a danger of imprisonment and other more general warnings. It was to be a dangerous time for us both."

"Did you look up the others?"

"No, but we didn't know the details of time and place of birth on the others. I admit we were interested."

"So was Maundy. And those details were on Cornell's desk. He copied them down, and he checked everybody else's horoscope to see what he could find. He even found an error in one of them."

"An error?"

"When he came here the other day, he was very excited and angry and nervous, and he let some things slip. He said Cornell couldn't even do horoscopes right. When I was at the hospital yesterday, Lane found an error that Cornell had made in one of the charts."

Koberberg said, "The only way Bruce could know about the error would be if he was the murderer!"

"That's right."

"Well, couldn't you bring *that* to the police?"

"Bring what to the police? I say Maundy said something that showed he had information that only the murderer could have had. Maundy says I'm a liar, or I misunderstood him. The fact he let slip is very small and very remote. It wouldn't be enough, not by a long shot."

"What if you talked to him again?" Koberg asked me. "If he's so excitable, he might make other slips."

"He already did. At least, I construe it that way. I've been told that Cornell and Dearborn never permitted anyone upstairs to their top-floor bedroom, is that right?"

"That's right. They both seemed to put great store in that, it was their private place."

"From what you said at Remington's the other night, I got the impression that even included people Dearborn would pick up while Cornell was away."

"That's right," Koberg said. "Cary told me that." He gave a sad little smile and said, "I got the impression half of Jamie's attraction for Cary was that private room. Cary wanted to see it, but Jamie would never let him go up there. Not for sex, not for anything."

"When Maundy was here," I said, "he said something about the drivers on the Brooklyn Bridge maybe seeing the murderer. That *might* have been said by somebody who'd simply had the room described to him, but it sounded like something said by a man who'd been there."

"Of course!" Koberg was briefly excited again, but then he looked cynical and said, "But that wouldn't be proof either, would it?"

"No, it wouldn't. My word against his again. And only a peripheral fact at best."

"It's enough, though," Koberg said. "Not enough to convict, possibly, but certainly enough to convince a sensible man. Bruce saw Ronnie's papers, and he'd been up in that room." He frowned and said, "But why do it all? I can see reasons for his getting enraged at Jamie, and after that killing I can see why he felt he had to protect himself by killing Ronnie, but why kill David? Why frame Leo?"

"He needed somebody to give Manzoni," I said.

"This is the second time you've mentioned Manzoni. I don't understand it."

I said, "As I told you Saturday night, it was Maundy that put the bug in Manzoni's ear about me. Maundy was in the car when I was stopped."

"That's right."

I said, "I'll tell you what I think happened after that. Manzoni wasn't one hundred percent sure of his position, and it made him nervous that Cornell was hiring people to snoop around. Also, I didn't give him much satisfaction, he was feeling a little frustrated when he left me. So he leaned on Maundy a little, I can guarantee you he did. It would be appropriate for his character."

"Leaned? In what way?"

"Pushed Maundy to find out why he was so set against an investigation. Warned him that if it turned out he was only trying to cover some wrongdoing of his own, things would get very rough."

"Yes, he would do that, wouldn't he? And Bruce wouldn't stand up to it very well; those superficially tough people never do."

I said, "Maundy was afraid my hanging around would either expose him or stir things up to the point where the police would take a second look at the case and maybe *they'd* expose him. So he figured he had to make sure things quieted down."

"By killing David and framing Leo? What a shabby reason to end a man's life and ruin another's."

"I suppose he would have preferred to kill me," I said, "but that would have opened things up, and what he wanted to do was shut them down. And when he'd checked all the horoscopes, there was Poumon's with a warning about violent death and an aerial accident. He found out that Lane was going to be at the hospital with Cornell all day, he called Ross, he hung around the apartment building, locked Ross on the roof, rang Poumon's doorbell, was let in, killed Poumon, and left. That open window was his only mistake, probably out of nervousness, but it wasn't a big enough mistake to cause Manzoni to think twice."

Koberberg said, "So what do we do now? It goes without saying, I hope, that I'll do anything I can to help. And so will Cary."

"I don't know what to do," I said. "I don't know what *can* be done." I was pacing the living-room rug, trying to think. For the first time in a long while, something outside my own head—other than my wall, or the sub-basement—had distracted me from myself. I became aware of that suddenly, and came to a stop, confused.

Koberberg misinterpreted my expression: "Have you thought of something?"

I feel I don't have the right to stop punishing myself, I thought. *What a fool.*

"Mr. Tobin?"

I said, "No, nothing useful. Excuse me a minute, I want to make a phone call while I think."

"Certainly."

I went out to the hall to use the phone by the stairs, and Kate emerged from the kitchen to say, "Would you like coffee?"

"Yes," I said. I remembered the number; I dialed it, and asked for Marty Kengelberg. Marty is an old friend of mine from the force, who kept on being a friend after Jock was killed. So far from objecting to my playing detective without a license, Marty had even once sent me someone to play detective for; a psychiatrist who was having trouble at a halfway house he ran for former mental patients.

Marty came on the line after a minute, and I said, "Hello. How are you doing?"

"Don!" he said. "Good to hear from you!"

I said, "This is Mitch. Mitch Tobin."

"For God's sake," he said. "Hiya, Mitch. You sound just like Don Stark. You don't know him, do you?"

"No, I don't."

"I never realized it before," he said. "It's incredible. What can I do for you, Mitch?"

I said, "How impossible would it be for me to get a private investigator's license?"

Happily, he said, "Mitch! You mean it?"

"I'm not opening an office," I said. "But just to have for self-protection, in case I need it."

He said, "Any pressure I can use to push it through, Mitch, you know I'll do it. Listen, it's been three years, hasn't it?"

"Twenty-seven months," I said. He was talking about my dismissal.

Ruminating, he said, "And you've helped out a couple of times since then. On that mob business two years ago, and the kid killed in the Village. I don't see why we can't get a couple of the right recommendations on it, and get it approved."

I said, "While the application's in process, can I practice?"

"That's a tricky area," he said, "but you could take a chance. I wouldn't worry about it."

"Good."

"I'll send you the form," he said. "You fill it out and send it back to me, not the address on the form."

"What if I come down there today and fill it out?"

"Even better."

"I'll see you in a little while," I said, and hung up, and went back to the living room, where I told Koberberg, "My wife is making coffee."

He was sitting in the same chair as before, perched on the edge of it, deep in frowning thought. He said, "If we could get Bruce to make some sort of move, if we could just get him active again."

"That's the problem," I said. "He's got things worked out so he doesn't have to move at all. The official investigation is closed, they've got their murderer, Maundy can just stay out of sight and the whole thing will blow over."

Koberberg said, "I keep wondering, what if we went to his mother? That's what he's been afraid of all this time, that his mother would find out. What if we went to her, and . . . I don't know what. Hinted at things?" He shook his head. "I'm not thinking rationally."

Suddenly a part of the conversation with Marty came back into my head, and brought with it a possibility. I said, "I've heard Lane do imitations of voices a couple of times. You once, and Remington. Can he do anybody else?"

"Cary? Yes, of course. He's very talented, as a matter of fact, he can do all sorts of people, the most astonishing things. Walter Matthau, believe it or not. Can you imagine Cary doing Walter Matthau? And Bette Davis, of course, and William F. Buckley."

"What about other people in the group, besides you and Remington?"

He said, "I really believe Cary could do just about any voice on earth, if he set his mind to it."

"You said before, he'd collapsed and he was at your place. What kind of condition is he in? Could he be helpful?"

"Cary would do anything to help at this point," Koberberg said. "That's what he needs, of course, something to do, something to take his mind off his troubles."

Like me? Kate walked in at that point with a tray holding coffee and cookies. We drank and ate and talked, and worked it out, and then Koberberg called Cary Lane and told him what to do in part one of the plan, and then we left for Manhattan.

21

I stopped off to see Marty and fill out the application form; a pink folder, it was, and half the questions set my teeth on edge, but I answered them. Marty wanted to know what I was involved with at the moment, naturally, but I told him I didn't have the time to talk to him right now, which was true, and promised to have him and Gail out to dinner very soon and fill him in then.

That was a strange moment, the first time in twenty-seven months that I'd invited anyone to dinner. I felt like a snake in the spring, just after shedding last year's skin: new, and raw, and cold, and strange, but somehow good, better than I'd felt in a long long time.

What had caused this change? I didn't know, and I was afraid to look at it too close, afraid it would vanish if I tried to touch it. The thought *I am happy* was still invariably followed by the thought *I don't deserve to be happy.*

We drove uptown, in Koberberg's roomy Jaguar sedan, to his apartment in the East Sixties, one of the most expensive sections of an expensive city. The block was similar to Brooklyn Heights in appearance, though somewhat wider and with wider and more obviously wealthy houses. We went inside, and I remembered someone having said this apartment was like living inside a giant plant. That was true; there were plants everywhere, from large rubber-tree plants in room corners that brushed the ceiling, to tiny ferns in pots on

end tables and the grand piano. The style of the place, what
could be seen of it through all the greenery, was traditional
and elegant, very different from the other apartments I'd seen
the last few days. I remembered that Koberg and Ross
were both interior decorators, and were in partnership
together, and I guessed that this living room was primarily a
reflection of Koberg. Ross would be less likely to devote
his attention inward at his own home.

Cary Lane looked almost normal. If he had looked, yesterday, as though the skull within his plastic face had been
removed, creating an emptiness into which his face was collapsing, today he looked as though most of that empty space
had been refilled. Not all, but most. There was still some hol-
lowness in his cheeks and around his eyes, but he did look
human again.

"She was home," he announced. "Bruce was at work, of
course. She said he'd be home around six, and I left the message. Are you *sure* it was him?"

Koberg answered. "We're sure, Cary," he said. "We
have to go down through the rush hour; if we're going to get
there before six, we'd better start now."

Lane put on a Dynel fur coat and matching hat and knee-
length boots with brass chains around the top, and we left.

The snow was coming down again in the same endless
slow windless fall. So far the city had managed to keep up
with it, keeping the streets clear, but it was piling up on the
sidewalks and roofs throughout the city, and every time one
went anywhere in a car it was first necessary to push a wet
heavy thickness of the stuff off the windshield; it was too
heavy for most cars' wipers to move against.

We were in stop-and-go traffic, with the wipers beating
back and forth across the windshield. Koberg and I were
in the front seat, and Cary Lane was in the back. He was very

agitated, and spent most of his time leaning forward with his forearms on the seat back between Koberberg and me. Finally, during the time we were on FDR Drive, he said, "This goddam snow! Doesn't it ever stop?"

"There's no wind," Koberberg said. "The same storm center's been over the city for a week."

"When does it empty, for Christ's sake?"

"I don't believe it ever does," Koberberg said. "It'll be blown out to sea eventually. When we get some wind."

The short days of winter are made even shorter by thick heavy cloud layers and steadily falling snow. We drove through an elongated twilight and an early night, the headlights of oncoming cars splintering in the water drops on the windshield. The interior of the car became too hot and stuffy, but when I opened a window a crack the air that came in was gravelike: damp and cold, reaching immediately through flesh to bone. I rolled up the window again.

We were stopped for a while in the Brooklyn-Battery Tunnel, part of an endless double row of murmuring smoking cars waiting like cows at milking time for the gods to solve whatever problem had arisen out of sight ahead. But then the lines began to creep forward again, and we emerged from the tunnel, and there was no sign of whatever the problem had been. There never is.

We had told Lane to call Jerry Weissman at Jammer, which he had done, and Weissman was waiting for us when we got to Ronald Cornell's apartment at ten to six. He buzzed to let us in, and when we went up the stairs he was in the open doorway, saying, "It hasn't rung at all."

"Good," I said.

We trooped into the living room. The one window shade studied us with an expressionless open eye, the other one closed its eye against us. The 747 still soared at us through a blue sky with puffs of cloud. There was still the feeling of floating, of no solidity; a queasy feeling.

I said, "Is there a second phone?"

Weissman said, "Upstairs."

"They both ring?"

"Sure."

To Lane, I said, "When he calls, answer immediately after the second ring, and I'll pick up at the same time. I don't want him to hear two separate clicks."

"All right."

Weissman said, "I've got the cassette."

"Fine." I turned back to Lane. "Are you all right?"

He looked pale, that was all. It was so difficult to read that face. He said, "I'll be all right."

"Do you want someone in the room with you when you do it?"

"I'll be better off by myself," he said. "Not so self-conscious."

"We'll all wait upstairs, then," I said. "Good luck."

"Thank you." As I started for the stairs, he said, "What if he doesn't call?"

I looked back. "He'll call. Maybe not exactly at six, but he'll call."

"All right." The voice was a truer witness than the face, and the voice was scared. Too scared to do the job? If so, there was nothing to be done about it. I nodded to him, and went on upstairs, followed by Weissman and Koberberg.

The phone was beside the bed. I took a fairly heavy book from the bookcase and put it in the phone's cradle, so I'd be able to work on the mouthpiece without a caller getting a busy signal. Then I got adhesive tape and cotton gauze from the bathroom and covered the mouthpiece so no sound from this room would be transmitted. Then I had Weissman show me the operation of the cassette tape recorder, a small compact machine containing its own microphone. Then there was nothing to do but wait.

We had turned on only the one light, a fixture that hung low on a maroon cord from the ceiling over the bedside table containing the phone. The light it gave was muted, and tinged with red. I sat there on the side of the bed near it, the phone receiver and cassette on the bed beside me, and I could look straight ahead at the wall of windows across the rear of the building, facing the lights of lower Manhattan. They seemed to wink and sputter tonight, like a guttering flame on the verge of going out, as the snowflakes descended and descended past them. And reflected in the glass I could see us shadowly defined: three men in a room where a murder had been committed, waiting for the killer to call.

22

The phone rang at twenty past six. I picked up the receiver
and cassette and held them close together in my two hands,
switching on the cassette. Weissman, standing beside me as I
sat on the bed, held his hand poised over the book resting in
the phone cradle. The first ring ended, after what seemed an
extraordinarily long time, and then there was a long impa-
tient silence, and then the second ring, again too long, and at
the end of it I nodded to Weissman, and he lifted the book
from the cradle.

The phone in my left hand clicked. A voice I didn't recognize, tinny and fey, spoke from it: "Hello?" From the way
Weissman's eyes widened, the voice I was hearing had once
belonged to Jamie Dearborn.

The other voice I did know: Bruce Maundy's. It said, with
fury and something else, "Who is this?"

"It's Jamie, sweetness." The cassette's tiny tape reels
turned, tape feeding through. I had thirty minutes on each
side, more than enough.

"I want to know who this is." Maundy sounded like a man
at the end of his rope. He sounded as though he might suddenly begin to pound the telephone against the wall.

"Listen, sweetness, I told you it's Jamie. Guess who's gone
to Atlanta?" The voice was seductive, arch, comic; a sexy
come-on combined with a sexy put-on. I was remembering
that Cary Lane had been one of the people Jamie Dearborn

had slept with during Cornell's visits to Atlanta; Lane was like this tape cassette, playing back conversations he'd had with the real Dearborn.

I felt a chill up my back. I *knew* what the situation was, I'd structured it myself, and still it was getting to me. How could it fail to get to Maundy, who couldn't know anything about the stage machinery, who had to recognize the voice, and who —even more important than the mere sound of the voice— had to recognize the things it was saying and the way those things were being said?

"I don't know who you are," Maundy was saying, gritting the words out, almost swallowing the telephone, he was crowding it so much, "but if I ever get my hands on you, I'll kill you. I swear I will."

"Oh, you already did *that,*" Dearborn's voice said carelessly. "Tonight, let's have fun. You know who misses you? Calcutta misses you."

There was silence, suddenly. I looked at Koberg, who had come over to stand beside Weissman and listen to the tinny little voices, his head bowed, his expression hooded. He met my eye and shook his head; he didn't know the reference either.

But it had caused an effect. It would be something sexual, then, some private joke that Dearborn had had with his lovers, something that Maundy would know but would associate with no one other than Dearborn.

"Brucy?" the voice asked plaintively, archly. "Bruty Brucy? *Et tu,* Brucy?"

"Where did you hear all that? Where do you know that from?" And now it was Maundy's voice I didn't recognize; it was hoarse, it trembled, it wasn't completely under its owner's control.

"Honey, you forget who you're talking to. *I* know my Bruty Brucy."

187

Lovers talk to one another in bed. Dearborn had talked, had told them about each other. At least, he'd obviously talked to Lane, with whom he'd probably felt more kinship than with any of the others. I doubted he'd talked about his other lovers with Cornell, and not much with Maundy, either. But he had with Lane, more than enough for Lane to be able now to pin Maundy to the wall and impale him there on memories.

Jamie the Jade, Koberberg had called him, and it was the jade I was hearing now, teasing, taunting, playing with fire.

Maundy said, "Stay there. Whoever you are, stay right there."

"Oh, I'll stay here, sweetness. You know what I'd like tonight?" And the teasing lilting voice suddenly got explicit, combining the bluntest of slang terms with arch private endearments, describing acts and positions and attitudes with loving care. And saying, "You know how I can turn you on over the phone. It's been a long time since I've done that, isn't it?"

"I'm coming there," Maundy said. His voice was trembling, but he didn't sound as though he'd been turned on. He sounded desperate, and deadly. "Wait for me, I'm coming there."

"I'll be waiting," the jade said, and there was a click, and the jade said, "Brucy? Sweetness?"

"It's over," I said. I stopped the cassette, and Weissman put the book back in the phone cradle, and the receiver became silent. I put it away from me on the bed as though it were unclean, and got to my feet, carrying the cassette. I wanted to walk, and there was nowhere to go.

Cary Lane came up the stairs. He looked as shaken as I felt. He said, "He's coming over." No questions about whether he'd done well or not; he knew he'd done well, and it disturbed him as much as the rest of us.

I said, "I know."

Jerry Weissman said, "That was the scariest thing I ever heard."

Lane said, "I wasn't sure I could do it. So I held one thing back, one thing that I would be the only one to know until afterward. To spur me on." He turned to me. "When I called Bruce's house and talked to his mother," he said, "she asked me if I hadn't called before one time. I was using Jamie's voice even though I didn't expect her to know it, just for the practice, and she asked me if I hadn't called before. And I said I thought maybe I had, and then I started to leave the name and number for her to give Bruce, and when I told her Jamie Dearborn, she said, 'Oh, of course it's you, I remember. You called just a few weeks ago, I still have the number you gave me.' And she gave me this number." He looked around at us. "That's why he killed Jamie," he said. "And David. To keep a silly secret that nobody ever even cared about." And as he stood there, the expressionless perfect face began to cry.

23

Had he become spooked? We waited, the four of us, in the big open top-floor bedroom, talking little, listening for the doorbell, and the time went by, and nothing happened. Even with the traffic, even with the snow still coming down, if he'd left immediately after the phone call he should have been here no later than seven. But then it was seven-thirty, it was eight o'clock, and he still hadn't showed up.

After his outburst, Lane had quieted down again, and he spent most of his time at the front windows, staring out at the roofs and the snow. Koberberg had delved into the low bookcase and was sitting now in a chair, idly turning the pages of books, but not really reading. He had turned the chair so his back was mostly to me, in order to get light on the pages from the one lamp we had burning, and I could see that his attention was only sporadically on books.

Jerry Weissman suffered the most from inactivity. He didn't feel right unless he could be actively helpful to somebody, and there was no help right now he could offer to anybody. He paced the floor, this way and that, in erratic random paths around the room, and from time to time attempted to engage one or another of us in conversation, mostly offering hopeful theories as to why Maundy hadn't as yet showed up. But none of us was very interested in talking, and the conversations all trailed off, and Weissman went back to his pacing.

As for me, I continued to sit on the edge of the bed, facing the rear windows and the snow and the flickering lights of lower Manhattan and the ghostly reflections of this room and us four. Sometimes I looked at the city, sometimes at the snow, sometimes at the stoop-shouldered reflected images in the glass.

I thought about Jock. I thought about him a lot, conversations we'd had, days of our partnership when specific things had happened. There was nothing homosexual between us, but there are other kinds of closeness that can become meaningful and real, and we had one of them. When I started seeing Linda Campbell, I never doubted for a second that Jock would cover for me, even though I knew he liked and admired Kate, and he did cover for me, without question, and thereby died.

And I died with him. When it became public that Jock had died because I had not been with him, and that I had been in bed with Linda at the time—whose husband I had four years earlier picked up on a burglary charge, back before the affair began—the mass of guilts had crushed me beneath their weight and I had simply died. But I had died in a way that had left it possible for me to feel pain, to ache with the memory of what I had done and the results of what I had done, so finally I had started my wall, to deaden the capacity for pain through physical work, to distract my mind from memory by filling it with simple questions of digging and building.

And whenever, in these two years, I had felt a thaw beginning within me—as on occasion I had—I'd always thrust it away again. My punishment was to feel guilt, to be as dead as Jock forever. Kate, who long ago had forgiven me, had remained sure that some day I would forgive myself, but I hadn't believed it. I had looked into myself, and I had seen no future at all. Nothing at all.

But suddenly this afternoon something had clicked into a

different gear inside my head, and all at once I had found it possible to permit myself reactions that were not colored by guilt. I had found it possible to think and act like a living man, to invite Marty and his wife to come to the house for dinner, to start thinking about tentative futures. And I was spending much of the waiting time now testing that new attitude, the way a man will flex a once-broken arm after the cast has been taken off. I thought of Jock, I consciously thought of him, recalled his face to mind, remembered how his voice used to sound—as Cary Lane had remembered Jamie Dearborn's voice—brought to the surface again whatever incidents of our partnership I could remember: good times, difficult times, pointless times, the detritus of memory. Checking myself for reactions. As Jock's surrogate, was I prepared now to forgive me, to declare my sentence completed?

I couldn't be sure yet. I only knew I felt the way a man feels after a long illness, just after the crisis point, when he is going to get better and knows it. He isn't strong yet, he isn't well yet, but he knows he's on the right road at last.

What I didn't know was the crisis point. What had caused this change, what in the last few days had unlocked my head? I had no idea. Eventually I might figure it out, but not yet.

And at twenty to nine the phone rang.

We all jumped. Reaching for the cassette and the phone receiver, I called, "Lane! Take it downstairs! After the fourth ring!"

"Yes!" He was already running for the stairs.

The second ring sounded. In the space between that and the third, I shouted at Lane, disappearing down the stairs, "Stay Dearborn! No matter who it is or what he wants!"

Had he heard me? The third ring sounded, so I couldn't tell if he'd answered me or not. And Weissman's hand was hovering anxiously over the book in the phone cradle. "One more," I said to him, and he nodded, his head movement jerky. Koberberg had gotten up from his chair and was coming over to stand with us, the book forgotten in his right hand, one finger marking a place I knew he cared nothing about.

Ring four. I hadn't started the cassette! I fumbled with it, agitated, and the fourth ring ended, and Weissman lifted the book.

The phone in my lap clicked, but the tape was moving in the cassette, everything was all right. I held the machines in my two hands, and brought them close together, and we heard that eerie voice again, Cary Lane with the voice of a dead man, saying, "Hello?"

"Hello yourself. Who *is* that?"

The voice wasn't Maundy's, but it was familiar. I looked up at Koberberg and Weissman, and Weissman whispered, "It's Stew!"

Remington? Dearborn's voice was saying, "Well, hel-*lo*, Uncle Stewart. How's Big Daddy?"

"My Christ, that's a good imitation. Who is this? Cary, is that you, you little bastard?"

Lane said something, gamely keeping up the Dearborn imitation, but it was no good. I dropped the cassette and yanked adhesive tape off the mouthpiece. I was too frantic, and it took longer than it should have.

Lane was still talking, but I broke in: "Remington, don't say anything. This is Tobin. Is Maundy on an extension?"

A short silence, and then he said, as though humoring someone, "Not at all."

"He can't hear me?"

"Now, you know that isn't so," he said, still as though humoring someone.

"Good," I said. "I'm sorry I wasn't smart enough to

realize he'd go to you. He's the killer. He fit Ross for the frame, and now the official investigation is turned off. We're trying to get him in motion."

"Are you sure it's me you want to talk to?"

I said, "You mentioned Lane. He'll remember now that Lane does voices, you'll have to cool him out on that. Can you dial this number again as though it were Koberberg's?"

"Yes," he said, but with some doubt in his voice.

"Remember that Lane's supposed to be at Koberberg's. Become confused as to who you're talking to here, maybe it really is Dearborn. Then tell Maundy you want to call Koberberg to see if Lane is still there. Call here again."

"Well," he said, "if you say so. Who *is* this, really?"

"Lane," I said, "take over again."

Lane's own voice came on the line, frail and frightened: "Oh, God."

Remington said, "Bruce is here. Why don't you talk to him, maybe *he* can figure out who you are?"

There was a little silence. I was holding the receiver down in my lap again, but holding it with two hands now, one palm over the mouthpiece. Koberberg knelt on one knee in front of me and held the cassette near the earpiece.

Maundy's voice came on, harsh and angry: "So it's Cary, is it? You're gonna get a lot less pretty, you son of a bitch."

"Oh, now, you don't really like Cary." It was the Dearborn voice again, effortless and smooth, still with the seductiveness in it, still without a quiver of nervousness. Lane could hide behind a voice as effectively as a face. "It's me you like, Brucy, and you know it. Except when I call your mama."

"I'll be seeing you, Cary," Maundy said, his voice heavy and dangerous, and there was a click as he hung up.

Weissman just stood there. I had to say to him, "Put the book back."

"Oh!"

Lane came up the stairs while I was fixing the tape and cotton back on the mouthpiece. I said to him, "You did fine. You and Koberg go downstairs. When Remington calls, you're at Koberg's place. Be ready for Maundy to get on the line."

"All right."

"Pick up after the second ring again."

"I will," Koberg promised.

They went downstairs, and Weissman said to me, "What's going to happen now?"

"I don't know. I was hoping he'd panic. He keeps being on the edge of it, but he just won't tip. It was bright of him to go to Remington, I hadn't expected that."

"Bruce is smart," Weissman said. "He acts like a hood, but he's really very smart. He's had a couple of one-acters Off-Off-Broadway."

"A playwright," I said. "That's right, I'd forgotten about that. Has a job in a ticket office to be near the theater."

Weissman gave a surprised laugh. "Not exactly," he said. Then he looked thoughtful, but didn't say anything else.

The phone hadn't yet rung. I looked at my watch, and waited, and looked at it again, and two minutes had gone by.

I got to my feet, leaving the phone mouthpiece and the cassette on the bed. "I'll be right back."

Weissman said, "You think something's wrong?"

"I don't know yet."

I went downstairs, thinking, *I handled this wrong. I don't want Remington on my conscience, too.*

Koberg and Lane were in the living room, under the

747, both looking worried. Koberberg said, "Do you think something happened?"

I said, "Call him. If he answers, play it that you're home, no matter what he says. This time Maundy might be on an extension."

Lane said, "*If* he answers?"

I didn't say anything. I kept looking at Koberberg, who stared worriedly back at me for an extra five seconds or so, and then abruptly sat down beside the phone and picked up the receiver and dialed.

Lane and I stood there and watched him. He was sitting there, very attentive, holding the phone to his ear as though it were telling him something fascinating. "It's ringing," he said, and that was the last thing he said till, "Ten rings."

Lane said, "It's only two blocks from here."

"Break the connection," I said.

Koberberg pressed the cradle button down with a finger, and looked at me.

I said, "Dial 911."

24

The police had gotten there first. A patrol car was out front, empty, its motor running, its red light looping and looping on the roof, the beam flicking through the descending snow.

The snowfall was getting heavier, denser, but still without wind. That had slowed the four of us, hurrying along sidewalks ankle-deep in wet snow, and it meant now that the patrol car's beacon hadn't produced its usual quota of spectators. Except for us, there were no other pedestrians on the sidewalk. Except for the patrol car, there was no other traffic on the street.

The front door stood open, the yellow corridor was brightly lit, the door leading to the living room at the far end of the corridor was also open. We went through and into the apartment, and I was struck at how large and empty and low-ceilinged it was. The only other time I'd seen it, during the party, it had been full of people and really very difficult to see.

The downstairs was empty. It was becoming weird; the intermittent blood-red light flashing through the front windows, tinging the green and yellow apartment, but no one to be seen. No Remington, no Maundy, no police. Finding nothing was almost the worst possibility of all; at any rate, the most frightening.

But then we found them on the second floor. I was leading the way, Koberg behind me, Lane and Weissman trailing reluctantly after, and upstairs I saw the library door standing open, and I walked down that way.

Two uniformed cops, both somewhat overweight, both wearing their slick raincoats. They filled the room, and for the moment they were all I saw.

And they both saw me. They frowned, and one said, "Can I help you?"

"I'm the one who called," I said. "Tobin. I gave my name." I walked into the room, and the other three waited uncertainly in the doorway. "Those are friends of Mr. Remington," I said.

"Do you want to tell us what happened here?" They didn't know the situation, and were going to be polite and circumspect until they got their bearings.

I said, "I'm not sure myself. Mr. Remington was here with a person we knew to be potentially violent. He was supposed to phone us, Mr. Remington was, and when he didn't we tried calling him and got no answer." I looked around, and saw legs extending out from behind the leather reading chair: someone lying on his back. I gestured in that direction and said, "May I—?"

"Sure," said the cop. He stepped back a pace to let me by.

I went over beside the chair, aware that Henry Koberg had come into the room now and was moving with me, and behind the chair Stewart Remington was lying on his back. One of the cops had taken the seat cushion from another chair to support his head. His face was battered and bloody, and the left sleeve of his maroon smoking jacket was dark with blood from the elbow down. His eyes were open, and his mouth twisted a little in a kind of smile. He said, hoarsely, "Well, Tobin, the banderillos are in."

"Are you all right?"

"I'd be better if I felt Bruce was going to be in any position to be sued."

Koberberg said, "What happened?"

"He saw through the phone call. I tried to keep him from seeing what numbers I was dialing, but it didn't work."

I said, "What did he hit you with?"

Remington coughed, started to move his left arm, winced. The cop who'd spoken before said, "Maybe he shouldn't talk now. We have an ambulance coming."

"It's all right," Remington said. "If I can remember to keep that arm steady. To answer your question, Tobin. Unfortunately, my faggotdom extends to a cane fetish. In a case downstairs. He took one and had at me."

"Downstairs?"

"I suppose I was to be another roof victim. He lugged me up the back stairs, but then the phone started to ring. He cursed and kicked me and dragged me in here, and then I heard him do a quick ransacking job in other rooms. To make me look like a burglary victim, I suppose. I expected him to come back and finish me off. I passed out several times, I'm afraid, and one time when I opened my eyes, the cavalry was here."

Koberberg said, "Stew, I think you should stop talking now."

Weissman had joined us, and was staring at Remington in horror. I had never seen them paired off together, as I'd seen Koberberg and Ross, or as I'd seen Lane and Poumon, so it came as a belated shock to remember that Weissman had been living here with Remington until this mess had started and he'd volunteered to assist Cornell. I said to Koberberg, "Why don't you take Jerry downstairs and have him make us all coffee?"

Koberberg frowned at me, mistaking the suggestion for obtuseness. "Coffee?" Then he got it. "Oh. Good idea. Jerry?"

"What? What?" Weissman was still staring at Remington, who now grinned at him and said, "Will you bring me hash in hospital, little angel?"

"Stew—"

Koberberg tugged at his arm. "Jerry, come on with me."

Weissman, his expression still stunned, allowed himself to be led away. Lane joined them, and all three went on downstairs.

I said to Remington, "You told the police his name?"

"And address and blood type," Remington said. "And I can't think *who* dear Bruce is going to get to represent him." The twisted smile showed again, and he said, "I believe I'd have to disqualify myself."

The cop beside me said, "I'd like to talk to you for a minute."

"Of course," I said. "But it will take longer than a minute."

25

I got a ride home on a snowplow. I'd left in Koberberg's Jaguar sedan, but by two-thirty in the morning, when I was finished at the precinct station, there were no vehicles other than snowplows still operating anywhere in the city. The snowfall, which had been persistent and steady for so long, had finally stepped up its pace and become a full-fledged storm. Still without wind, the snow was coming down now so heavily it was impossible to see more than half a block through it. Streets were impassable, subways weren't running anywhere that there was exposed track, and it was clear now that the whole city was about to be shut down for a couple of days.

Koberberg and Lane and Weissman and I had been taken to the precinct to tell our stories, which we did, to a team of detectives new to us and new to the case. I told it to them straight, leaving out nothing, and when I was done, they went for a conference with the lieutenant who was the acting chief of detectives when the captain was off-duty. Then they'd called the captain, who lived out on Long Island and who couldn't get in, and who didn't like the thought that something might be about to blow up in his face. They put me on the phone to him to tell the story again, which I did. One of the detectives was on another phone, and when I was finished, the captain said to him, "Is Manzoni on duty now?"

"No, sir. You want us to call him?"

"No. I'll see him tomorrow. You handle it, Bert."

"Yes, sir."

"And make sure we're doing it right this time."

"Yes, sir."

They'd already sent to pick up Maundy on the assault charge. I'd expected they'd find him at home and that he'd deny everything, and both happened. He was brought in and told of his rights and elected to remain silent, and was put away in a cell for the night. I told one of the detectives, "As soon as he realizes this means his mother will find out, he'll try to kill himself."

"I know," he said. "We'll be careful."

In between each period of action or talk there were long silent spaces of waiting, Koberg and Weissman and Lane and I sitting on wooden benches along one wall of the bullpen. There was very little activity other than that concerned with us. For some reason, I found it easier to be in this setting this time; it seemed more comfortable somehow.

Weissman kept calling the hospital where Remington had been taken, and finally an intern gave him a report, which Weissman repeated at happy length; it was full of contusions and abrasions, with the compound fracture of the left arm as the worst injury, and nothing that was even remotely fatal.

Maundy would have to explain, himself, why he didn't finish the job and kill Remington, and I doubted he ever would. But there'd been blood on the stairs he'd dragged Remington up, and maybe he'd realized he couldn't make a suicide leap from the roof look sensible this time, so he'd changed his plan to burglary-with-murder in midstream. The phone ringing must have rattled him, and he'd ransacked the place first, leaving the death of Remington till the end. But then, I suppose, the patrol car arrived, and he went out the back way as the cops were coming in the front.

In any event, the assault charge was enough to hold him on for tonight, and tomorrow morning—or whenever the snow permitted—a real investigation into the Dearborn and Poumon murders would begin. I had no doubt that convictable proof would be found without too much trouble. Maundy had run into luck in the person of the investigating officer, Manzoni, but he had needed luck: his manner was too abrupt, his methods too erratic, his cleverness too improvisational. He hadn't done clean methodical work, and now at last professionals would begin to look for the flaws.

It was two-thirty in the morning before I left the station. A detective drove me through just-cleared-and-already-filling-up-again streets to a Department of Sanitation garage, where a route was worked out that would get me home, eventually, after traveling on three different snowplows. I spent an hour and a half high up in the cabs of the yellow plows, listening to the tire chains rattle, seeing the mounded white landscape the city had become, and at just after four I made my way slowly through snow higher than my knees up to my front door.

Kate had left lights on in the living room and kitchen. I considered whether I was hungry or not, decided I was too tired to be hungry, switched off the lights, and went upstairs and to bed. I fell asleep almost at once, and I dreamed that Jock called me on the phone. I still couldn't make out any of the words he said, but he didn't sound angry. It was amazing.